WARRIOR OF RIGEL

Airship 27 Productions

Warrior of Rigel
©2024 Gary Lovisi

Published by Airship 27 Productions
www.airship27.com
www.airship27hangar.com

Interior and cover illustrations © 2024 Ron Hill

Editor: Ron Fortier
Associate Editor: Gordon Dymowski
Marketing and Promotions Manager: Michael Vance
Production Designer: Rob Davis

ISBN: 978-1-953589-81-1

Printed in the United States of America

10 9 8 7 6 5 4 3 2 1

WARRIOR OF RIGEL

GARY LOVISI

PROLOGUE:

As I walked through the magnificent ancient city of Vorba, marveling at its beauty as it sat like a gorgeous jewel upon the gleaming waters of the Great River, I entered a less than reputable eating house to feed my raging hunger. Upon entering the establishment I took a seat at one of the many small tables, while the other numerous, and rather unsavory customers, eyed me curiously and with obvious avarice. Newcomers were always suspect in a place like this, and often the victims of thieves and rogues. I made sure my sword and dagger were easily accessible should I need them.

Suddenly a bull-headed fellow flung back his chair and walked towards me with deadly avarice and violence in his eyes. He was a bold rogue who I could plainly see was planning to take me down right there in the tavern, to rob me most likely, if he did not kill me, but I was ready for him. He quickly drew his sword, but mine was already out. He cut a swath at my head just missing my face, but my blade made a cut that cleanly loped off his right ear. He screamed loudly, but no one came to his aid. In a place such as this, the other denizens of the place only laughed and looked away. The man bled profusely and quickly ran from the room in pain and anger. I knew he was gone for good and would not return.

I sat down and appeared to relax, but remained alert for any action.

"That was Lanka, a piece of trash who seeks out easy prey, which it appears you are certainly not," the man at the next table told me with a winning grin. "We are better off without him. That was good sword work."

I nodded, cleaned the blood off my sword and sheathed it, but kept it ever ready. "I am no one's prey at all."

"I see that," the man smiled, then he looked away and continued with his meal. I kept a wary eye on him, and all the others in the place.

"What shall it be?" a greasy-faced waiter asked as he ambled up to me whipping my dirty table with a rag that was even more dirty. He did not mention the fight at all. I noticed this was not the cleanest place to dine, but at least it had a reasonable menu of what went for food in such a place. A twisted half moon smile appeared upon the man's bloated face as he looked me over with a greedy gleam in his bloodshot eyes. I knew that look well. Lanka had it, and he had paid, so I could see this fellow was much more careful.

"So what will you have?" he spoke up slowly.

"One roast *osk* leg and a mug of your best ale," I replied, all the time thinking

5

about departing the place for a cleaner establishment, and bemoaning the fact that I was here on a mission, and here was the place that fortune had led me.

"Quickly, young lord," he responded as he waddled away and into a back room, for he could easily tell that I was an Asudran lord, being one of the nobility and powerful of the world or Rigel, no matter my disguise. That was not good for me.

I was ravenously hungry, and while waiting for my food I chanced to look around the room more closely to examine my surroundings, checking the appearance and danger of my dinning associates. Instantly my eyes fell upon a young, well built warrior who looked familiar to me. His back was toward me, so I could not see his face, but he appeared to look remarkably like Baldar, an old friend.

As I watched the man, I saw him get up from his table and throwing a few coins on the stained wood, he began to leave. He still had his back towards me. Only a true warrior however, would have felt the eyes of someone watching him. Cautiously I watched as he slowly turned to have his gaze fall directly upon me, his right hand moving quickly but unobtrusively to the hilt of his long sword should there be trouble.

The warrior carefully turned towards me now. He stared at me intently. I gasped and gave him a friendly smile. He returned it. I was correct, it was Baldar. Instantly I recognized the man's face as being that of my old friend.

"Baldar!" I spoke up in surprise getting up to greet him now. "Whatever are you doing here of all places?"

He appeared just as surprised to see me, as I was to see him.

"Ah, so it is truly you, old comrade!" he blurted happily shaking my offered hand now in greeting. "How are you my friend? It has been a long time."

"Yes, surely it has," I replied with a genuine smile. It was good to see the fellow after so long. "So much time has passed. So how are you? How are things back in your city?"

"I was just going to ask you that same question. What are you doing here? Why are you not back in your home city of Asudra?" Baldar asked curiously now.

I sighed softly, "Come sit down here with me and we shall talk," I said offering him a chair at my table.

As he sat down at my table, the waiter brought over my food and drink. Baldar had already eaten, but he was never one to turn down a free flagon of ale, so we ate and drank as we spoke.

"So old friend, what in blazes are you doing here?" repeated Baldar, his friendly good-nature was like a long missing sight from home. "And why are you not in Asurda?"

I nodded grimly, "Well, now, that is a long story. Have you the time?" I asked trying to hide my anger and memories about all that had happened to me in the past, but it was a boon to my heart to see this old friend again and to be able to tell him of my many terrible travails.

"I have nothing but time, especially for an old friend. Now tell me, what happened? We shall drink and talk, all night if necessary. Why do you suddenly appear in this city? You seem to be dressed as a common warrior and not a nobleman. I know something is up."

"Well then, since you asked, then I shall tell you," I spoke up marshalling my thoughts. "My uncle, Azare, emperor of Asudra sent me upon a simple mission of peace, or so I thought, but it turned into one of war and revolution. He said that my journey would eventually make me a true warrior of Rigel, but I had no idea at the beginning of my quest what it would turn into. It had to do with an evil noble lord who ran a world-wide outlaw cult known only as Zorr. He had taken the name of the Rigelian god of the Underworld, and was the cause of much misery for me and those dear to me. Are you sure you want to hear of it?"

"Of course, Tan, tell me all about it" Baldar replied happily. "I have nothing but time for you or such a story."

I smiled, saying, "Very well then, my friend. Here it is."

CHAPTER 1

The strange story I am about to relate began one day a long time ago. I, being a prince in the house of Alvaka, of the imperial city of Asudra, was sent north by my grand uncle, Azare Alvaka, the emperor of that important and powerful city-state on the planet Rigel. With a few loyal armed men I was to travel northeast to the city of Aboola. Recently Asudra and Aboola had been in a bloody war, but that war had not gone well for either side in that too-long conflict. Perhaps Aboola had received a much more bitter piece of it. I was to go there and try to effect terms for peace, if it was at all possible. It was what we all hoped would be a blessing for the people of both war-weary city-states. For the world of Rigel is littered with many powerful but self-sustaining city-states constantly at war with each other.

I left my city with a dozen stout and brave Asudran warriors as escort, my ambassadorial bodyguard. Three *talas* later I found myself in the eastern territory of the notorious Zunds. These are a wild and untamed tribe of violent savages, some of the cruelest inhabitants who roam the vast plains of the world of Rigel. It was ominous, for no sooner had my small party entered the Zund country, did I notice two silhouetted figures far away who were apparently following us across the sand dunes.

"Zunds, My Prince, probably scouts from a war party," Soth, the captain of my bodyguard, who was riding at my side, warned me quietly. "We should be cautious and quicken our pace, for even though we are well armed, our small party could be attacked. These fiends are ever war-ready."

I nodded, he was certainly correct. "Have the men alerted. We will proceed at a more rapid pace."

With the Zunds at our heels things looked like they were taking a bad turn. Even though it appeared there were only two of them—where there was *one*, there could be a hundred—where there were *two*, there could be a thousand. So it was surely a bad turn of events. How bad a turn of events it would prove to be for us, I would not realize until later.

It might have been possible from the outset for us to go around the territory of the Zunds, by not crossing into their lands at all, but I was in a great hurry and that would have taken us far out of our way. Lives depended on my embassy. I decided to take the shorter route, perhaps against my better judgment.

Many *tals* later my small party rode northwest. We were pushing our ponderous *zibas* for all they were worth, the huge wooly mounts moved quickly for their great size. I noticed we were still being followed by the two Zund outriders. Soon we slowed to a normal gait, Captain Soth not wanting to weary our mighty mounts in case we were attacked and needed to rapidly flee. Our huge *zibas*—the large ponderous dray animal used everywhere upon Rigel as beasts of burden of all kinds—as well as cavalry mounts were moving quickly. They could move quickly when properly motivated. They were nervous. Each of the huge shaggy beasts—six-legged mammoth-sized mammalians—moved most carefully and quickly for such apparently slumberous beasts. Although they were huge, many of the younger ones were also slim and sleek so that the *ziba* can be quite a fast running animal when necessary. It is also generally a well-tempered brute. I say generally, with caution. The creature has two rows of large flat teeth in its cavernous mouth, and if left to its own devices will munch the sweet grass of the endless plains of our world forever. While not often of a mean temper, they can be bred and trained to have a mean disposition for war. In fact, many a warrior has been injured by his own savage mount's foul temper, which can flare up at times for no apparent reason. While a raging *ziba* will not only sometimes kill his own rider, it may also go on a murdering rampage. It takes a strong warrior to be able to control these brutes.

As we moved on, our Zund followers continued to track and watch us. Then I noticed there was another group of men to the north. This was a large grouping of perhaps a hundred mounted men, and there was something that was strange about them. As they came closer, I was able to pick out individuals more clearly. That they were Zunds, there was no doubt. That did not bode well for us, but as I watched they were now completely encircling some other group of five other warriors. These may have been the scouting party of riders that had been following us for so long. Instead of attacking my party, this new group of Zund warriors attacked this party of five—who I could now see were *not* Zunds!

The five warriors were fighting bravely and taking a terrible toll on their Zund attackers, boldness and bravery seemed their battle plan, but I knew eventually they must succumb to the greater number of attackers surrounding them and moving against them so forcefully. Their time was running short.

I have found in life that it is interesting why I do certain things. Why I take a certain action. Perhaps I was heartened by the bravery of those five defenders—perhaps it was time for me to take some kind of action to help them? I can not say why, but I did not like to see such brave warriors in a weak position being so hard pressed upon. So I gave the order to Captain Soth to rally our warriors and ride forward at attack speed to the aid of the five defenders. Soth was a good man, and I had chosen him as captain of my small party for that very reason, but at my order he quickly rode up to me and caught my attention.

"My Lord, I know not what you are doing," he told me cautiously for his mind was on the purpose of our mission and not on saving some careless travelers or desert nomads. "Your reason to help these five truly is in the heart of all the men here, and myself also, but you must remember you are on an important mission for the emperor. If we are defeated, or captured by these merciless Zunds, we shall never reach Aboola. That means the war will go on and many more thousands of people will be killed."

"Yes, we are all brave men," I said realizing my error, but I could not deny the call of a greater duty. "No doubt, the mission is always upon my mind, Soth. However I am torn between my duty and a greater call of honor. How to decide? I will tell you what I decide. We must help those desperate men—so let us ride now!"

"Yes, sir, where you lead, we follow," Captain Soth replied with a sharp salute.

"Then so order the men," I told him crisply.

Just at that moment one of the captain's men came alongside Soth.

"Captain, we have spotted another group of about one hundred Zund warriors behind us. They're coming up fast—at the charge."

I noticed the newcomers now and nodded, "Captain Soth, tell the men to draw their swords and follow my lead. We go to fight against the Zunds and save those five brave defenders!"

With swords drawn and with bold war cries shouting out over the roar of our mighty steeds, we charged towards the scattered and unwary Zunds. My men and I were upon them before they knew what was happening and cut a wedge of blood through the surprised enemy until we rode through them and reached the beleaguered defenders. Only three of which were still alive and mounted.

At first the Zunds were taken aback by our sudden attack and faltered for a moment, but once they realized there were only a scant dozen of us, they regained their bravery and with their greater numbers came at us with a renewed fury. In the first minute of the attack, three of my own men, brave souls all, went down. I noticed that another of the original five defenders also went down. The battle was brutal and furious. The Zunds were blood hungry now and realizing we were outnumbered, regained their usual semblance of bravery. I now recognized the defenders were from the faraway city of Cathor. Whatever were they doing here?

The battle raged on, mounted men on enormous raging *ziba* mounts, flashing swords cutting a swath in blood and gore. We fought bravely but were terribly outnumbered—and that fact did not sway the Zunds but only emboldened them. They saw their chance and took it.

Soon the second Zund war party we had spotted moved closer. They had seemed to be so far away, but now had arrived and joined the battle to fight beside their comrades. Now it had become a terrible bloody melee. The enemy were coming at us from all sides. Soon there were only five of us left alive. We fought in a tight mounted square, which made it more difficult for our enemy to approach us. If we were not all proficient riders, we could never have been able to control our massive and brutish mounts, but we held them in a masterful defensive line to hold off the enemy. Our bloody flashing swords did the rest. For the moment.

The Zunds were not as proficient riders when battling mounted in such close quarters. So our strategy saved us for the moment, but we knew it could not last. We found ourselves now outnumbered by ten to one, and though we had given a good account of ourselves, I saw the remaining two Cathors who fought so bravely, soon cut down. Now it was just myself, with Captain Soth, and another, who fought desperately for our lives, trying to take as many of the vicious Zund warriors as we were able down with us into the night black land of the dead. For now it seemed death awaited us all. So I gave a lusty growl that this seemed the end of Prince Tan Alvaka of Asudra, and my mission. Nevertheless, I fought on and made my enemy pay for every sword stroke they came at me with. My two companions gave as good as they got as well.

Suddenly the Zund chieftain ordered his men back away from us. The enemy gathered together and moved off. Soon we three survivors remained mounted alone in the center of a large ring of enemy corpses and leering blood-thirsty Zund warriors.

"Surrender now! You shall become slaves, but you will live," the Zund chief told us with a vicious twisted smile. I was most curious by this offer. I had never heard of them taking prisoners, not even as slaves, but apparently they did so. "Surrender or you shall die a useless death."

We were given a few moments to decide. Soth and I debated what to do. It was not any kind of good decision either way. Death—or slavery among the Zunds. That life as a slave might be worse than death—and even as I had those thoughts I still had my mission to think of. That meant that we had to live. I had to stay alive. Somehow. That was the key to my choice. Quickly the three of us agreed there was nothing we could do but surrender. Instantly the three of us were disarmed and bound tightly as captives. To become Zund slaves.

We were tied behind two large *zibas* and dragged behind the massive animals. The Zunds noted that one of the Cathor defenders was still alive. It seems he had only been knocked unconscious, so he too, before he could act, was disarmed and bound with us. Now all four of us were tied together with ropes connected to the horn of the Zund chieftain's saddle. Then we were herded to the east, much to the cajolement and laughter of the barbarous Zund warriors, who lost no opportunity to kick and spit upon us, very much enjoying our captivity.

That was a dark time for each one of us as we silently endured the degrading action of our captors, which each of us knew would be much worse once we were under the full control of our merciless enemy. We were all silent and sad at our failure. The warrior from Cathor was brought forward and was tied behind me and I took the measure of the fellow. He seemed a strong fighter and he had proven his bravery. I began to engage him in conversation. Naturally, I was curious to discover who it was who I and my men had aided, even if it was apparently now at the expense of my own demise. We both began to speak.

"I must thank you, sir," the young Cathor spoke up softly, so the Zunds would not hear him. "Who are you? What city are you from?"

"I am Tan, Tan Alvaka of Asudra."

"Well, I am happy to have met you, though I wish the circumstances were of a more amiable nature. I am called Hotath Zel, I am from the city of Cathor."

It was a simple enough introduction between two men who would soon become fast friends and fierce comrades in arms.

CHAPTER 2

It took many *Talas* for us to get to the main Zund encampment. Hotath Zel and I spoke constantly, closely held as prisoners on the trip. It seemed we had much in common. I found him a forthright, simple but honest man. I felt that I could trust such a fellow and when at the mercy of the vicious Zunds, it is good to have a companion you can trust.

"So you are a prince of Asudra?" the Zund chieftain asked, he had evidently overheard Hotath and I speaking. "Perhaps it is a good thing I did not kill you, for you may have some value, perhaps even bring me a high ransom."

I just laughed at him, and he jerked on the rope roughly throwing all four of us prisoners onto our faces and then dragging us in the dirt. He and his warriors laughed at this heartily, thinking it very funny. The highest level of sport in the Zund world, abusing prisoners. They were a cruel and nasty lot. It took a while before all four of us could stand up upon our feet, as their mounts continued to pull us roughly behind them.

I quietly told Hotath of my peace mission, and that caused him to look at me gravely. He realized the importance of such a mission, but seemed to be dubious of the outcome now.

"Those from Aboola are a strange breed of people, they are ruled by a madman," Hotath told me candidly. "Cathor is also at war with them, and I was also sent by my emperor to expedite a treaty of peace with them as well. I entered Aboola with a one hundred man escort, and left it with only five—only after a heated battle and a swift escape. Obviously they did not take kindly to our peace mission, even as they misled us with their intentions. Perhaps you would have had better luck, but I doubt it. Then we escaped Aboola, but fell prey to the Zunds. Afterwards you and your men came to our aid."

"Why would the Aboolas break their truce and destroy their own chances for peace by warring on two such great powers as both our home cities? They are a smaller city, warlike yes, but not stupid. It does not make sense," I asked curiously. "Do they have a suicide wish of some kind?"

Hothah shrugged, as if to say who could figure an enemy?

I said, "so you believe if my group had arrived in Aboola we would have also been attacked and killed?"

"Absolutely," Hotath replied confidently, "and they would do it in the most cowardly manner. Do you know they lavishly accepted us into their palace, then they tried to murder us all in our sleep?"

That news did shock me for it is only a vestige of a man, and the lowest coward at that, who would seek to murder anyone in his sleep. It seemed Aboola was full of treacherous low mannered fiends with no honor at all. Perhaps that was from the most common warriors right up to the very emperor of the city itself. Nothing breeds hatred like dishonor and treachery.

"Did you ever meet with their emperor?" I asked Hotath.

"No, but I saw something much more significant," he replied quietly, with a tinge of an enigmatic tone.

"Well? Do not be shy now, my friend. What did you see?" I wondered, prompting him to speak up.

"It was most perplexing. Their previous emperor, although a young man was said to have been murdered by an assassin from Cathor. That I can tell you is an out and out lie. Anyway, I never saw this new emperor who has taken his place. He would not see me. I only saw one of his ministers. Well, that fellow proved to be a most arrogant bore who thought so highly of himself it was the height of arrogance. He scoffed at my idea about a plan for peace between our two cities, telling me that soon Cathor will come under the control of someone he spoke of mysteriously as Zorr. Whoever this Zorr may be, I do not know. I have never heard of him. Whoever he might be, he takes the name of the god of the Underworld—the evil 'Dark One'. I assumed at the time that he must be the new emperor of Aboola, but now I am not certain. He wore a black hooded robe and his face was covered with a hideous shiny mask. Have you ever heard of him? Or any such men as these?"

I shook my head thoughtfully, "No, I think not."

Then Hotath continued, "In any case, my men and I were taken by the minister's major domo and given quarters in the palace to sleep that evening. There, in the middle of the night Aboola warriors stealthily entered our sleeping chambers. They took out my sentries. They carried drawn swords and daggers, and came at us in a killing frenzy we had never seen the likes of before. They had already murdered a dozen of my men before we fully realized the vile treachery. Although I was highly suspicious of the Aboolas, I *never* dreamed they would stoop so low as to send men to murder me and my companions in our sleep! We were furious! My men and I fought well and gathered together into a group where the enemy could not take us down. Moments later the battle was done, most all my men, except five, were killed. Then I saw a way for us to escape the palace. After running down the hallways of that labyrinthine building, we stopped fast and remained silent when I heard suspicious voices coming from a private chamber through a crack in the door."

I nodded listening intently as Hotath continued.

"Quickly I motioned my men to be silent as I looked into that room, for I was intently curious about what we had stumbled upon. Here was some secrecy I was sure I needed to know about. There were only two men in that room. One seated in a chair with his back to me who I could not see, the other man was the very minister to the emperor we had met earlier that day."

"The very same! So what was that all about?" I asked eagerly.

Hotath continued with a grim smile, "The minister spoke to the man in a most differential tone, as if he was some kind of lackey, which seemed most unusual for such an arrogant type and so highly placed as he appeared to be. But what he said most differentially and with almost slavish demeanor was his use of the title Zorr, the same name as our Underworld god. He did not say it as if the man were 'a Zorr', but as if his very name was 'Zorr'. It seemed inconceivable. This I believed was the source of all our trouble. Then I saw the man known only as Zorr hand the minister something. I saw that it was some kind of gold ring, but I could only see it for a brief moment, then the minister placed it upon his finger."

"Did you ever find out who this Zorr might be? What of his name and city? Why the mysterious black robe and mask? And what is that ring for? And why use the name of the god of evil and death?" I asked curiosity fairly bursting out of me, for it seemed that we had not heard the last of this fellow and he could be serious trouble for our people and our home cities. Here seemed a sudden and treacherous danger, but what did it really mean?

Hotath took a deep breath and continued, "All I know is that the minister put the gold ring on his finger, and this Zorr told him he was to wear it always—for it was most important to show his stature in the organization. What 'organization' I had no knowledge of. Then I pushed open the door, and with my men we charged into the chamber. The room was a large and well appointed palace chamber, and immediately my drawn sword was met by the minister's own, who turned out to be an excellent swordsman. Meanwhile, the man known as Zorr was nowhere to be seen, he had seemingly disappeared into thin air. The man named Zorr was quickly gone from the room, and later I found he had fled behind a curtain and somehow escaped through a secret passage. I would have liked to unmask that one. Anyway, the minister and I fought and though my men tried to capture him for questioning, he surprised us all by taking his own life. Most surprising, from such a man possessing no honor, let me tell you. The minister cut his own throat right there in front of me. I tell you it was a ghastly scene."

"Rather than be captured, or surrender?" I asked totally astounded by the man's shocking tale of suicide.

"Yes, most strange. So very extreme, and that is not all. When I looked behind the curtain where this Zorr had disappeared, I found there to be a solid wall. I know not how he did it, a secret doorway of some kind no doubt, but I had no time to search for a lock or any mechanism, for just then the palace guards were coming. As we left the chamber, I remembered the gold ring that I had seen Zorr give to the minister. I quickly stole it off the finger of the dead minister. Then we fled. Eventually we fought our way out of the city and made it into the desert, where we eventually fell into the hands of the Zunds."

"Well, that is quite a story. And quite a mystery. I wonder who this Zorr is and what his game might be?" I mused. I had not heard the name before in relation to a man, only a god. Perhaps, he too thought he was some kind of a god—whatever the reason his use of the name seemed very significant.

"I do not know, Tan," Hotath replied thoughtfully.

"You think he might be this new emperor of Aboola?"

"I am not sure."

I nodded, it was a nice mystery to ponder, but I and my companions had bigger problems to worry about. Noticeably I needed to escape from the Zunds. And that might prove to be the most impossible feat of all.

That night Hotath Zel, Captain Soth, and I, as well as the remaining warrior who was called Hupa, were chained to a large tree in the center of the Zund camp. When everyone was asleep we quietly came to life to discuss our plans in silent whispers. We had to figure out some means of escape. None of us relished staying as captives of the Zunds, so we tried to perfect a plan for freedom. Since both Hotath and I had an important mission, it was decided that I should go to Aboola, while he would go to his home city of Cathor to make his report.

However, I saw an equally important need that we find out all we could about this man called Zorr, and the meaning of that gold ring. What was his plan? What was he up to? It could not be anything good. This all seemed to be somehow intertwined with Aboola and the war with my home city of Asudra. Therefore I changed my plan and decided to go to Cathor and try to find out what information I could. From Hotath's words, it did not seem that I would be much welcomed in Aboola in any case. Hotath Zel decided to go to Aboola. Hotath saw the key to all this mess as being created in Aboola. I was not so sure, but I respected his judgment.

"You, Prince Tan, should go to my home city of Cathor and seek out my family. I have a plan. Let them all know that I am dead—at least publicly," Then he gave me the gold ring—the Zunds had not found it in their cursory search—and he told me seriously, "you must carry this gold ring on you and try to seek out other members of this nefarious cult, secret society, or whatever it might be."

Hotath gave me the gold ring and I put it on my finger. It was large and heavy, no mistaking that it was solid gold. I nodded, then told Hotath, "Good, I will take care of that and see what I can discover. Captain Soth, Hupa and I shall go south to Asudra. There they will alert the fighting forces of my home city to aid us, if we should need them. I feel there are dark forces afoot, and we have merely touched the tip of some great mischief that lays underneath."

"And I have a most ominous feeling about this Zorr," Hotath added with concern, then his expression brightened. "However, I am happy to find out that I do not stand alone in this."

"You are not alone, my friend," I told the warrior from Cathor, and I offered him a grim smile. "We just have one slight problem. I hardly feel it worth mentioning among all our grand plans and schemes, but, well… just how do we escape from the Zunds?"

Hotath laughed, "That is a good question, Tan," he replied as he returned my grin. "I believe it should not be too much trouble for a royal prince of Asudra to come up with a more than adequate plan of escape. After all, you are a noble prince of a powerful house, while I am but a poor and lowly warrior of no great influence and education. A person of no consequence."

I could scarce repress my grin of amusement at his words. No matter what Hotath Zel told me I could not picture him being merely some poor lowly warrior. He had regal and royal qualities of true leadership. Later, when I asked him about this, he told me the strange story of his life.

"Once, a long time ago," he began sadly, "the House of Zel ruled Cathor, but dozens of years ago there was a revolt. It was against one of my esteemed ancestors called Sar Zel. Maybe you have heard of him?"

"Yes, I have," I replied shocked that such a bloody despot could be related in any way to the brave noble warrior who stood before me.

"Yes, indeed," Hotath continued with little pride now. "We Zels contain the royal blood line of Cathor, but my family revolted against Sar Zel. You see, Tan, not even clan loyalty could bind us to a man with such lust for hate and bloodshed. He was eventually overthrown, another took his place on the throne, but this time it was not one from the House of Zel. Soon the Zel clan became the scorn of Cathor, prosecuted and hated, blamed as the cause of all the cities troubles. The Zels are not popular in Cathor even to this day. I am the male heir of the once proud Zell clan, one remaining lowly warrior, with nothing but a sharp sword and proud memories to assuage his thoughts."

I hardly knew how to respond to all that, so I did not. I think Hotath appreciated my silence and I kept it for a long while. Then we began to talk of other things.

We sat there talking all night while our Zund hosts slept soundly and snored loudly. Some Zund warriors were on guard, but they were far from us. Nevertheless, we were too securely bound to attempt any possible escape.

"We must do something quickly," Captain Soth told us in a low tone. "In a few *talas* we will be at the Zund encampment in the Hills of Mystery. There can be no escape for us then."

Hupa shook his head fearfully, "No escape for us at all."

I nodded my agreement. We were silent, trapped, bound and helpless. It was not any kind of good position for us to be in. At the moment, no plan that had any measure of success presented itself. We were too carefully watched, hard-bound, so we had to be content to bide our time and look for some opportunity—any opportunity—however slim to present itself to us for escape.

The next *tala* we were once again all tied to the line and secured to the saddle horn of the Zund chieftain. There seemed nothing we could do to change our predicament.

It was the four of us against over a hundred vicious and well armed Zund warriors. I knew we had no real chance, but I still would never gave up. We had been traveling for half the *tala* when we suddenly saw a small caravan coming out of the north. It was probably coming from out of Aboola. Instantly our captors, behaving as Zunds always behave, prepared themselves for an attack on the outnumbered and helpless caravan. They smelled riches and plunder—and battle!

I knew this must be the chance we had been looking for. I alerted my companions. It turned out that we were quickly left behind with only three burly mounted and most reluctant Zund warriors to guard us. The rest of them went charging away led by their chieftain, with swords raised and war cries voiced as loud as possible to attack and capture the Aboola caravan. The promise of loot and killing lusty upon their lips.

"Here is our chance to escape!" I whispered conspiratorially to my three companions. I knew it might be our only chance that we would ever have. My companions agreed and we set about to make the most of the situation.

All three of our Zund captors were busy watching their brothers as their mounted charge quickly rode down upon the caravan. Our guards cheered their comrades, but also cursed them, since they were not among them to share in the spoils. They quickly broke out drinks and then had much argument laying wagers as to how much time it would take for their comrades to destroy the Aboola caravan.

The Aboolas did their best to defend their caravan, moving the wagons and positioning their own scant amount of riders to meet the Zund attack. They were brave, but there did not seem to be enough of them. Nevertheless, the fight was furious.

That was just what I wanted to see. I slowly and cautiously approached the back of the biggest and the most formidable Zund. His giant *ziba* mount grew uneasy as I moved close but this captor was much too engrossed in the battle to respond to what his mount was trying to tell him. I quickly crept up upon him, and because of the way he was seated upon his mount, I instantly noticed his dagger tilted back, half out of its scabbard. It was most reachable by me. Here was my chance and I took it!

I grabbed the large bladed weapon, carefully and quietly easing it out of the scabbard as my companions looked on watching me nervously. They were ready to come to my aid in a fight, if it should come to that. Suddenly I saw the huge Zund move into another position. I quickly placed the dagger into my

"HERE'S OUR CHANCE TO ESCAPE!"

harness and pretended to be engrossed in watching the battle that was now going on in full warfare—though I always kept a wary eye on the three Zunds. The one I had taken the dagger from had not noticed his loss—not yet—but he turned around and looked at me comprehendingly. Suspicious coward.

"Trying to sneak up on me, ah you Asudra filth!" he barked loudly.

His two companions merely looked over at me and grunted, sure that their friend would make quick work of me—but not kill me—as I was a valuable captive. For now. I moved away slowly.

"I was merely watching your brave brothers being defeated by a small detachment of caravan guards—not even proper warriors! It is a shame!" I replied somewhat acidly.

This made him laugh and he gave me a sharp kick in the back, sending me flying far behind him. "Stay with the other prisoners, slave!" Then with a grunt he turned away from me and continued to watch the battle with his other two companions.

This is just what I needed. He would regret that kick, for he had sent me right beside my comrades and in an instant I had the dagger out and had cut lose all their bonds. Now all four of us were free—and we were ready for battle and vengeance!

With a silence and care borne out of skill we fell upon our three inattentive Zund guards. They had never expected such an attack.

Of course, they were armed and we were not, but we had the element of surprise and we used it most effectively. We came at them so quickly that the three of them were dead before they knew what hit them. I made good use of that dagger by returning it to the gullet of it's former owner. Meanwhile my three companions quickly took down the other two Zunds so that they soon resided in the shade land of the dead. Surprise was written large upon their slack faces in blood. Their own.

Quickly Hotath and I each seated ourselves upon our captor's massive mounts. Captain Soth and Hupa shared the remaining *ziba* between them. Before we rode off we took a moment to take in what was happening at the battle at the caravan. I realized that it would be quite a while before the Zunds were finished. Eventually, they would surely win and capture the caravan and kill or enslave all it's occupants, but unlike most times they did not greatly outnumber their enemy so much this time.

Quickly the four of us looked at each other and nodded at our alliance. We were free now. We had already made our plans to go our separate ways as to that plan. Hotath going north to Aboola; Captain Soth and Hupa traveling south to Asudra; while I headed southwest to Cathor, the Glittering City of Jewels. In a flash we were off.

CHAPTER 3

A s I estimated it, I was perhaps two *talas* from Cathor in time, so I wasted no effort in making my way there. The first *tala*, that day and night, I was alone. However, tasting the sweet flavor of freedom, though it was uneventful and I was by myself, was clearly wonderful. I had escaped the terrible Zunds, and so was careful to lay low. I did not want to encounter anyone who might interfere with my mission.

It was on the afternoon of the second *tala* as I raced south on my mighty mount, when I soon noticed there were riders following me. At first I thought they were another tribe of Zunds, but eventually as they came closer and caught up with my tired mount, I saw they were dressed far too strangely to be those nomadic warriors. Then who were they? And more importantly, what was their intention? I tried to outrun them but my worn out *ziba* was just too tired to keep up a rapid pace for much longer.

As the riders came closer I could see that they were garbed completely in long black robes which concealed their entire body. That was most strange. Their heads were also hooded in black. I counted twenty of them, ominous looking figures to be sure. As they rode in closer I saw that the only ornamentation they wore was a mask covering their face, a black harness with a sword and dagger, and a necklace of some small brown baubles of some kind. As they approached I noticed those baubles seemed to actually be round disks of some sort. The disks were brown and some of the riders wore more of them that others, some having what appeared to be an entire necklace made of these strange brown disks. When I could see them more clearly, the images on their face masks were utterly hideous, twisted and most fearful. Obviously they had been created to instill as much fear in their enemies as possible. I knew that, so it did not scare me—but I was surely concerned by it.

One of the approaching enemy—for I was assuming they were such—the man who I judged their leader—seemed to have almost a hundred of these disks in a long necklace around his neck. They were strung from rope or wire that led from shoulder to waist. However, at the moment, I did not think about what this might mean. My one concern was who these strange riders might be. And what were their plans for me? For I realized that there was no getting away from them now with my tired mount—and there was no way I could fight and prevail against so large a number of warriors.

Once this group of twenty mysterious robed riders rode up close to me their leader drew his sword and approached.

"Submit!" he ordered simply. There was no debate about it.

"So then, that is the way it will be! So be it!" I blurted defiantly, as I in turn drew my own sword. I quickly turned my mighty mount to meet his own head-on, determined to sell my life dearly.

Then I noticed that the strange brown disks these mysterious riders wore, were not disks at all—but shrunken human heads! They were clotted with dried blood which gave them their brownish color. This produced a most ghastly sight as the enemy came at me wearing these hideous trophies in full array and their gruesome terror masks of metal showing horribly distorted faces. No one could view them and not be unaffected. Then in a heartbeat they were upon me, but it was not unexpected. I actually surprised them by coming back at them hard and fast, my flashing sword blade wove a path of crimson death among them so they became very wary of going up against me. They moved off, then rebound and came at me all at once, trying to surround me.

The battle raged furiously. Quickly I dispatched three more of the enemy riders when the leader, so bravely standing *out* of the fight, ordered all his men to rush me at once again. I knew I could not hold all of them off for long as they moved to surround me, and soon I was trapped, held at sword point, and quickly disarmed. I was then thrown from my mount and held firmly by four of the men. Almost immediately their black-hooded leader withdrew a long *osk* hide whip. I saw that two other of his warriors did the same. The leader gave the order and instantly one of the whips fell upon me stinging me with searing pain and rage.

Instantly I stood up and lunged for the closer of my attacker's throat, pulling the whip out of his hand. It was a brave but useless gesture I knew, for no sooner had I hit him than I was knocked back down and then tied to a stake with two swords at my throat to temper any future struggles.

"Now you shall learn obedience!" the leader's voice growled at me from behind his hideous metal face mask. "We shall tear every inch of flesh from your bones. Then we will leave your remains for the ever hungry *xos* to feast upon."

I swallowed fearfully now. That was something I had not figured on. The *xo* is a large ravenous insect living all over the plains, and they are particularly fond of human flesh. They attack a man by the hundreds in huge uncontrollable swarms and can devour a full-size man in but a few *bans*. They can devour a huge adult *ziba* in five or ten *bans*—in just a heartbeat! Thinking these thoughts filled me with sheer terror—but at least I knew that oblivion with a swarm of *xos* would be swift. My heart trembled at this thought of death, of going into the afterworld in such a manner. It was not a warrior's death at all.

That was just the point and it angered me more than I realized.

Then the same man that had captured me, whipped me as I was tied down to the ground by his comrades. He and his comrades laughed with glee anticipating what was to come. I wondered just what was to come, but I did not have long to wait at all. For at that moment I spotted one of the dread *xo* insects come out from it's hole in the ground for exploration. It must have been a scout of some kind, moving towards me to investigate what had been stripped and tied down helpless in front of it. It moved cautiously forward, then came on faster. I knew it would soon see me and smell the scent of my blood and fear, and it suddenly let out a low screech in anticipation of it's grizzly feast alerting the *xo* swarm. Soon the *xo* scout was walking with it's insectoid legs up my own leg, crawling upwards upon my body while I now spied another of it's kind coming closer to me.

I was tied so securely I could not even shake the loathsome creature from me. The masked leader of these fiends laughed at my plight, and I could hear him cracking wicked jokes to his men. Then his men got together and took out silver coins to bet on how long I would last the *xo* attack. Then the whip came down again upon my back. The whip cut brought up more blood, and that seemed to work the horrible insects into an eating frenzy as many more now poured upon me and soon would be all over me. I knew the bite of the fiends would begin in a matter of moments measured in heartbeats.

I closed my eyes in utter despair and defeat. This was it then! I knew now that I would never reach Asudra again. What of my peace mission? It was over and done. It grieved me to fail in my duty. It did not grieve me to die, for everyone must die sometime—I just preferred that it would be at a later date in time and not in such a horrid and painful manner. Not to be helpless and eaten alive by a ravenous *xo* swarm. I shuddered to think of the next moments, the next crack of the whip, and the vision of hundreds of frenzied *xos* eating me alive.

Already half a dozen of the horrible creatures were crawling over my legs and moving upwards towards my arms. Now all feeling in my limbs was gone, for the *xo* have a paralyzing toxin they inject into their victim before they begin their grizzly feasting. I could feel nothing. It was most unusual. Then I did feel the sting of the whip upon my chest and next one of the loathsome creatures was moving inexorably towards my neck. I looked upon it with a macabre fascination. It almost seemed as if the monstrous insect was smiling at me, and at that moment I thought I should die of fear and terror.

Then the creature bit me and injected some of it's toxin into me and instantly I found myself fighting unconsciousness. I raged. I could not fall into unconsciousness now! Otherwise I would never wake up again! I tried to fight it. Then I heard the crack of the whip again and that is the last thing I remember as I stoically accepted sweet oblivion.

When I awoke the first thing I saw was the horrid hate ensnarled mask of one of my attackers looking curiously down at me. The masked face was not the same one as the previous leader. This seemed to be someone else. I looked back up at him and growled in rage and defiance.

Then this man did the most surprising thing. He bowed, and spoke nervously, "You will live, Master. I got to you in time. I am grievously sorry, these foolish men did not notice your ring. I assure you your punisher has been put to death—the same death he had proscribed for you."

I could hear a man screaming in the background and wondered what it all meant.

I stared at this new masked man in confusion and shock as I tried to sit up and figure out what had happened. I noticed that my wounds had all been cleaned and bandaged and that this new warrior leader had called for hot food and cold drink. He ordered his men to bring it to me and they placed it down before me with fearful respect.

Now I looked at this new leader carefully and noticed a copy of the same ring upon his finger that I wore. Yet, his was made of bronze, while the one I wore was made of solid gold. This new leader seemed to grow exceedingly nervous and seemed to even tremble a bit in front of me. Why I did not know, unless my ring proved that in some way I was of a higher rank or order than himself in this secret organization of the ring wearers. Zorr. What did it all mean?

I later learned this was true. There were iron, bronze, silver and gold ring wearers. The gold was worn only by members of some group called the High Council. High Council of what, however, I did not yet know.

"I offer my most abject apologies, Master," the man told me once again in a placating voice that almost begged for mercy. "I did not know. I could not have known. Please spare me."

Then the man surprised me by going down to his hands and knees and begged in terrified fear for his miserable life. His men stood by silent and fearful. I hardly knew what to say or do about any of this this. I did know one thing, that I must play along, and find out as much information as I could—for my life depended upon it.

"Master, I did not know it was you," he told me now with a show of true fear. It seemed my silence put more fear into him than any rage or anger I could ever have voiced against him. "I will be your loyal servant always. Please, enact the boon of pity."

I didn't know what to do, or to say at that point, but I knew I had to start thinking fast. I had to come up with something…

This leader's men were standing by silent, fearful, thoughtful. Waiting. Finally they began to grow bold and then laughed, making sport of him and his dire situation. It was obviously his action against me had created a bad reversal for the man—and his men were enjoying his terror and evident downfall. Perhaps they moved up in rank if they took down the leader in rank above them?

I did not feel sorry for the black hooded masked leader.

When I asked the leader why he had not killed me, he told me it was because I wore the ring and he feared all who wore such a ring—especially the Ring of Gold.

It would have been better off for him to have had me killed, but I did not tell him that. Then with me dead he would not have to fear me, or my revenge. When I hinted this to him he and his men fell back in terror, some actually shaking nervously. Their fear was genuine and I wondered what could put such terror into these brutal and deadly nomadic desert men. It gave me much cause for thought and concern.

Then all of these brutal warriors—who I knew gave way for no man— suddenly all bowed down and chanted: "We are forever loyal to our leader who knows all and is all powerful! We reaffirm our allegiance to our Master! The true one—Zorr!"

They chanted this mouthful of tripe continually and fearfully together three times. I was quite amazed but said not a word. Then they continued, "Forgive us, oh master Zorr, for attacking one of your beloved servants. We knew him not."

So now I knew that this so-called Zorr, who I had just heard tell of, and this group of secret masked hooded warriors and killers, were somehow connected. How they were connected, I did not know yet, but I would strive to find out.

Then the masked and hooded figures stopped their chanting and their leader once again—a man not used to begging—begged me for his life.

"Mercy," he asked softly in remindful worry.

I was about to say something when suddenly another of his own men came over to the man and kicked him full in the face, sending him reeling backwards a dozen *haads*.

"Kill the creature now, Master!" this man told me. "It was on his order we rode out to capture you, and it was under the order of his second in command to torture you. That man is no more. This one must die!"

"Why?" I asked, my mind awhirl at all this news. Then I allowed a grim smile and told them all, "Not one of you stopped him or came to my defense. Did you? Not one of you noticed my Gold Ring—and that is your true crime."

They all seemed shocked by this outburst from me and could not look me in the face.

Then I stood up and shouted loudly so all could hear me, "You are *all* guilty! Did any of you help me? No! You should all be put to death! But fear not, if you obey me now."

Every warrior grew suddenly quiet. I saw hands move slowly to swords. I may have pressed them too far.

Then pulling a bluff I said, "I know that Zorr does not continence incompetent fools!"

All of them were quite nervous now and looked at me sheepishly. I was sure that they didn't know what to do with me. I am sure some wanted to kill me outright and bury my body in the sands and be done with me—but once again, too many witnesses. I am sure many thought saving my life was a mistake, yet none so far had said it. I began to ask them many questions in a manner to mask my ignorance, but I soon found that neither I nor they knew who the mysterious Zorr might be. I asked why he took the name of the Rigelian god of the Underworld—and none could tell me—or would tell me.

"You, if anyone, should know who Zorr is," their leader finally told me allowing his suspicion to now show through. "After all, you are a Gold Ring wearer."

I thought fast, and replied by telling him, "That is a funny notion. You know that Zorr always wears a mask to hide his true identity."

This seemed to satisfy him and his men for the moment, as I saw many heads nod, but they were still uneasy and all wondering what I would do next—and what they would do next as well. I let them stew a bit, then looked into each of their faces and nodded. It indicated mercy. I saw many of them breathe easier. In this way I dispelled their fear of what I might do—or order—and I am sure I saved my own life by indicating to them that I would forgive their perfidy, if they would escort me to the stronghold where their leader, this Zorr fellow, held sway.

"That is wise of you, My Lord," the leader told me, his fear now abated. His name was Droth, and he was noticeably relieved. "We were on our way to the Hills of Mystery when we came upon you."

"I see," I spoke up thoughtfully. It had become quite dark. It had become very late. "Then we shall leave first thing in the morning."

We made camp and went to sleep, except for some posted guards. As I lay in my blanket I could not help thinking of my luck in this *tala's* events—saving my hide—and now leading me possibly to the answers I sought. So the stronghold of this secret society was in the Hills of Mystery? I thought it seemed a fitting place for a band of outlaws and cutthroats such as these. No one ever traveled through those bleak hills for fear of outlaws and brigands, slavers and killers who controlled the vast territory, because it was such an easy area to defend against any invaders. It was not under the rule of any civilized city-state and so was entirely lawless.

As I lay in my blanket, I pondered my fate about the next *tal's* adventures and what that day might bring. My thoughts also wandered to how Hotath Zel was doing and if Captain Soth and Hupa ever made it to Asudra safely. By this time on the next *tal* I hoped to have this so-called Zorr unmasked and his entire secret cult, that was set against the free cities of Rigel, broken. At least I had high hopes for such an outcome. As I fell into a dreamless sleep that night, tightly wrapped in my blanket with a dozen death cult cutthroats sleeping on all sides of me. I kept a ready hand upon my sword and dagger.

CHAPTER 4

The next morning we were up early and soon mounted, racing north towards the deadly lands that make up the Hills of Mystery. Droth, who I discovered was the equivalent of a captain, had learned nothing of my secret. Neither had his men. For that I was much relieved. To them all, I was seen as a powerful Gold Ring wearer, a man high up in the secret society of these outlaws, and that was all. It seemed I was a very important man in this cult of killers, to be much respected, and feared, a close servant of the man who called himself Zorr. Soon I hoped to unmask that mysterious and dangerous secret terror.

We had been riding north for the entire *tala* and soon reached the lower land that led up to the Hills of Mystery. As we neared the area I dismounted and prepared to walk with my mount upwards towards the hills, but the others stayed mounted. When I asked Droth why his men held back, he looked at me suspiciously, then his face changed and he gave me a grim half smile.

"You are such an important man in this society, My Lord," he told me in what I thought sounded like an ominous tone. Then he added, "You see, we are only mere warriors; servants who must obey Zorr's laws and ride our mounts inside the stronghold so we are always in plain view of the guards."

So they have laws and a structure. And guards. Guards, he had told me, though I did not see even one as we drew closer moving into the hills. In fact, nowhere did I see anyone at all in those tall grasses, thick-bole trees, all-covering shrubs, and then mounds of large rocks. There was no one to be seen here. Or was there?

We had walked quite a while and suddenly from above our heads atop a tree, a man's voice called out to us. A man we could not see.

"Enter through the south entrance," his voice told us simply. "A Gold Ring wearer is expecting you."

"All right," Droth answered and he led us to the opening.

"What news have you, friend," the guard atop the tree shouted down to us and now that we were closer I could finally see him. He was a small man, but looked well armed and suitable to his task. "Did you kill the emperor of Aboola?"

"Yes, he is dead," Droth told him, oozing with malignant pride, "and Crovis has now been installed as First Minister of the city."

Crovis was dead! Of that I was certain. I smiled grimly to myself, relieved that Droth did not know this news yet, nor did the stronghold guard apparently.

I knew that was true because I now wore the Gold Ring previously owned by Crovis. Taken off his dead finger. If they knew this, then they would surely wonder why I—a Gold Ring wearer—had been alone on the empty plains. Then they would surely suspect I had killed Crovis somehow and taken his ring, and was using it now as a spy. I smiled grimly, assured that my health would take a sudden turn for the worse if such were the case. So far they did not know anything about any of this and I hoped it would stay that way.

As we passed the guard, I saw that he noticed me and looked upon me most curiously. I got a very cold feeling as we moved forward.

"Droth," the guard asked, "I see you have a Gold Ring wearer with you."

Droth nodded.

Then to me, the guard spoke up, "Master, Zorr himself is coming here tonight for a meeting of the High Council."

I nodded, and cut in quickly, "That is why I am here."

That was the only reply I could give at the time, but I said it in such an arrogant manner as to shut down the inquisitive nature of this guard. He knew better than to ask anything more. Too many questions, and too much inquisitiveness, was a good way to get yourself a quick death among this group of scoundrels.

We proceeded towards an area he indicated and had gone no more than a short distance from where the first guard was stationed, when we reached a group of large trees that were just ahead of us.

"We are here," Droth spoke up. "The southern entrance."

"Good." I said bluntly, but I did not see any entrance at all. Ahead were only a thick wall of trees that seemed to go back into a bleak forest as far as the eyes could see. However, I did not let on to Droth about my confusion. I just looked forward and said, "Now let us make haste."

"We must wait, Master, for them to open the secret portal," Droth replied dryly.

That kept me quiet, and I let out a quick, "of course," even though I could see no entrance or portal, as Droth had called it. I wondered just what might be up. Could they be testing me? I grew nervous but kept my outward calm, looking at my companions closely. There were a full dozen hearty cutthroats, so it would be a tough battle should it come to that—and a battle I could not win against them all. I sighed, then said to myself, so be it. I was ready for whatever would be put to me and I would meet it the best I could, with a stout heart, and a sharp sword blade. I was a warrior of Rigel and would never go down without a fight.

Then I did see something so bizarre it made me think I was having some kind of delusion. For as we approached the tree line of the vast and thick forest, the very trees seemed to be uprooting before my eyes and falling off backwards away from us. It was the most inconceivable thing. Then with amazement I realized I was looking on a huge portal opening downward into the very bowels of the Hills of Mystery.

It was an enormous entrance, large enough to allow ten riders abreast to enter. We rode onward, and found it dark and grim, as we dismounted and walked our mounts inside and downward on a degraded slopping walkway. At the end of this was a brilliantly lit corridor with more guards in the familiar black hoods and capes.

As we neared these guards one of them in charge ordered us, "Identify yourselves!"

Droth raised his hand and showed the ring upon his finger, "Bronze Ring, Droth, and I am here with a Gold Ring wearer who is to meet with the Master."

The guards nodded, and their chief said, "There is a High Council this evening."

Then the guards took Droth's mount and my own, and the two of us left the group and were led into an adjoining corridor.

Here Droth and I were brought before the man who wore the Gold Ring being the commander of the stronghold in the Hills of Mystery.

We were in a large chamber of extravagant beauty and lavish furnishings. I was in awe that such a palace could be secreted here within this grim wilderness, deep in these underground caverns far below the Hills of Mystery. The new leader who also wore a Gold Ring, also wore a golden face mask, with a hood and robe of black that completely concealed his identity. He gave off a most ominous appearance.

As we went further into the room he looked up from his desk and told us to enter and be seated. He was a large man of middle age and bore numerous scars from combat that I could see upon his exposed arms and legs.

"What is your report, Droth?" this Gold Ring wearer asked, evidently recognizing my companion though he still wore his own robe and mask of concealment.

"Yes, Master," Droth replied with the proper amount of differential subservience. "I have brought with me a Gold Ring wearer I and my men found stranded out upon the plains. He ordered me to bring him here."

"I see," the Master spoke up softly, without any other comment or question.

Droth seemed very ill at ease, in fact I assume that he was terrified that I would tell this Gold Ring wearer what conditions of torture he had placed me through. However, he had no worry of my saying anything about that. If I did speak up, Droth would surely receive a most horrible death at the hands of these masked murderers. Worse yet, it might cause some embarrassing questions asked of me that I could ill afford to answer.

"Ah, I see, so Gold Ring wearer," this leader said to me—he was also a Gold Ring wearer, so we were of equal rank, "You came here for the High Council this night?"

"Of course," I said in what I hoped was a firm voice.

"Good."

Quickly I nodded.

It seemed as though he smiled suspiciously, though of course I could not see his face.

"Is Zorr here now?" I asked boldly.

"Of course not," he told me in a short impatient tone. "You know better than that. He only comes before the High Council just before each meeting and he leaves immediately afterwards. I find it suspicious that you were found alone in the desert. Why is that? If you are indeed a Gold Ring wearer, then tell me, what city do you hail from?"

I remained silent and motionless, thinking what I would say to that question. I was thinking furiously, and I think my questioner was doing so as well.

Droth looked on curiously, but wisely did not utter a word.

Then the man added, "You can not be our Asudra agent for I know him well.

Personally. What city are you from and why are you not robed and masked? And where are your bodyguards?"

I nodded, smiled, and tried to bull this through, thinking it was my best course to reply by speaking up boldly, "I am not robed nor masked because I am a spy on a special mission for Zorr. I have important news for his ears, and his ears alone!"

This seemed to quiet the Gold Ring wearer. He seemed to think about this and finally replied, "So be it. We have few quest quarters here. You will stay in a room with Captain Droth. Do these conditions meet with your approval?"

"Yes," I replied dryly, then looked closely at the man, and added, "for now. However, I need to have free movement throughout the stronghold. I am a Gold Ring wearer and must have my freedom in this place."

The man behind the desk just nodded, then gave us a motion of dismissal.

That was fine with me. I wanted to see what his response to that demand might be. It was obviously a delicate situation for him to be in. I didn't like the idea of Droth keeping so close and always looking over my shoulder. It did not seem likely that I should see this Zorr in a private audience. I had waited a long time for this meeting so that I could stop this upstart tyrant and his secret cult of outlaws and killers. At the time, I had no idea how deeply rooted and deadly this cult actually was—and so extremely powerful.

Quickly Droth and I left the commander's chamber as others came into the room with their own business for him. I tried to listen in as we left but could not make much out of what was said in the quick moments before we had to leave the room and the door was closed behind us.

Droth and I were escorted to our quarters. We were led through long corridors and I became even more amazed at the size and enormity of this stronghold. It was a vast underground fortress, a maze that was the size of an entire city, and seemingly populated with a large populace of assorted accomplished thieves and cutthroats. Eventually we reached our quarters and Droth and I entered the small but adequate room.

I began to take stock of my situation. It did not look good. I tried to make some kind of plan about what I would do—and how I would get out of this. I knew I had to find out who this man called Zorr might be, so I had to play the game a bit longer before I could even contemplate an escape. I looked over at Droth. And what was I to do about him?

For the moment there seemed nothing I could do, for I found the door to our chamber locked. Obviously my story was not as much believed as I would have liked it to be. So I just curled up on a bed and tried to sleep. I saw that Droth took the other bed and was asleep in moments. At least Droth and I got some much needed rest.

Soon afterwards we were awakened by guards. As we dressed they waited to escort us to the Great Hall where the High Council was to meet. I took my time, still trying to work out this situation in my mind. In the time that I stayed with Droth I pegged him for a coward and a liar, just as all the members of this secret society seemed to be. Or so it seemed to me at the time. They were the worst of the worst. Yet, there was something special about this fellow Droth that I could see when his guard was down. He did have a vestige of honor mixed with a great fear of authority. I imagined. Or some fear. Obviously well-founded in this grim place. Authority encompassed especially by myself, who he thought to be a Gold Ring wearer and a powerful representative of Zorr himself. I decided to use that for all it was worth. Droth told me constantly that he regretted that I had almost been killed, and he was both delighted and curious when I had not told the stronghold commander all that had happened.

"I do not understand your reasons for being silent about all that happened between us," Droth said carefully, "but I thank you for that silence. I tell you now, that forever after, my sword shall always be at your side, Gold Ring."

I nodded, thanked him, told him I appreciated the support, but wondered how he would feel if he knew that I was a spy and not any Gold Ring wearer at all.

Then he asked me what my secret mission for Zorr had been. I was surprised by this questioning, as it seemed to be more than mere curiosity. It had me wondering about him. Was Droth put here in with me to spy upon me? Was he suspicious of me? Perhaps even a spy himself?

I looked at him firmly and spoke rather sharply, "You know, this spy business must be kept silent and secret. I am sorry, but I can not tell you anything. That knowledge is for the ears of Zorr only."

Droth nodded, accepting my explanation.

That forestalled further inquiries upon that subject.

Soon the guards came for us. After we left our room we were led down a long well lit guarded corridor. Our escort, a taciturn fellow named Grazat, led us but said not a word. He took us down another corridor and then one other, the end of which I could see two large doors. Soon these doors were opened. Grazat, motioned for us to enter, but he did not. I was accompanied by Droth into a large hall of immense proportions. It seemed to be hand hewn entirely out of solid rock. I wondered who could have built such a place—surely not this band of criminals and killers. Or could they? Did they have that kind of power and organization? I wondered just what their game might be. Who were these people? What was their intent? I hoped that soon I might find out all about it.

"The Great Hall," Droth told me with pride as we walked inside. It was a splendid chamber, a palace fit for a king. I now reassessed the power of this secret cult. They had immense power—secret power. Droth then continued, "I have only once been admitted to the hall, and never the High Council. I wonder what news Zorr has to tell us."

As we walked into the immense chamber I also wondered.

CHAPTER 5

The Great Hall was truly immense and I judged that it could hold tens of thousands. The carved stone tiers were arranged in a vast semi circle around a permanent center created for the speaker so as to be heard loud and clear—I assumed that speaker would be whoever this Zorr might be.

Close to the far wall was a large throne apparently covered completely in gold. It was a fitting seat of power for a king who ruled a vast and secret empire. I was impressed and grew very fearful for this was an organization of great wealth and power. They were very dangerous and needed to be dealt with.

As Droth and I sat down on the hard stone seats, I noticed that many other men were now pouring into the chamber from various entrances. I assumed when all were present, mighty Zorr himself would make his presence known. No doubt from the heavily guarded door behind the golden throne. When it appeared that everyone had entered the meeting chamber, the Gold Ring commander of this secret fortress stood up from his seat in the first row and called out for silence before Zorr made his appearance.

Suddenly the door behind the throne opened and flanked by a dozen guardsmen and important looking officials, was the man who I assumed must be Zorr. He made his entrance like a king. Or dare I say it—a god! As he did so, drums and horns celebrated his appearance and soon everyone in that magnificent hall was standing and cheering in abject respect. Or was it from deep-seated fear? All of the most important higher level men were masked, the regular warrior's faces were not masked but only showed abject fear and obedience.

As far as I could determine the man called Zorr was completely covered, concealed so well that I could never determine his true identity. He wore a golden robe and a mask of gold that was shaped in the most grotesque twisted

"THE GREAT HALL." DROTH TOLD ME...

face of what looked to be pure rage and hatred. A terrible visage I had never seen before. It said plainly to all—obey!—and expect no mercy!

This Zorr seemed to be a creature of the very incarnation of evil to my senses, so he was well named after the vile god of our underworld. I could sense my feelings about him were not far from the truth. He looked out among the throng of his servants—slaves all to him certainly—with an insecticide precision as though they were the meanest of lowly creatures. Glaring pure evil emanated from him, even though his face was always covered. His voice and words sent a chill into every man there—and these were the worst fiends the world of Rigel had to offer. They did not scare easily. However, they were terrified of this human manifestation of the god of the Underworld and death.

When all there were enwrapped in a chilling silence, standing motionless as a statue, the man known only as Zorr stood up and prepared to speak.

"My loyal officers and warriors, our Secret Society is making victory after victory in our plan for world-wide domination across the cities of Rigel. Already our agents have assassinated the emperor of Aboola, a short-sighted man who would not accede to our demands. Now one of our own men, by the name of Crovis rules there for us. Others of our agents are gaining power in the cities of Vorba, Asudra, and Bovar to the south. Also, the Zels of Cathor, have finally been expelled from that city. They were our greatest threat there. Soon my brothers—we shall control all the powerful cities of Rigel! They shall be under our power and serve us all!"

There were resounding cheers and raised voices of victory.

Then the man known only as Zorr suddenly left the chamber to raucous wild cheering and rampant shouts of victory. It seemed all those attending the brief ceremony were awed and rapturous of their leader—and some no doubt greatly feared him as well, but all there obeyed him. It was a strange relationship. These men of the Hills of Mystery throughout time immemorial had always been criminals, thieves and killers. Assassins on a grand scale. However, there were also others running and hiding out here, men who had been unjustly accused or judged guilty of crimes in their own cities. Whatever the reason, these men had never before had anything in their lives. Now thanks to this Zorr, it appeared they would soon own a world. I shuddered at what they would do with it, if their plans came to pass. I knew I had to stop them, but that was easier said than done.

However, the prospect of stopping these fiends to me looked grim indeed. This Society of Zorr apparently had agents in every city on the world of Rigel, and even inside my own beloved city of Asudra. Other powerful cities as well. And now I learned that Hotath Zel's family had been exiled from magnificent Cathor. I realized that Zorr did hold considerable power and he posed a terrible threat to the freedom of all the civilized cities upon my world.

I sat there pondering the events that had just passed and what I might do about them, when the commander of the stronghold called his men to order with a gruff oath.

"All Gold Ring wearers must proceed to the council room where the High Council shall begin their meeting," he ordered, and the men began to rise and leave. "All others must leave here and go about their business. Raiding parties for Cathor will form outside at the Southern Portal."

Quickly everyone left to go to their assigned points. Droth also got up making ready to leave, telling me he had to meet others for that very same raid upon Cathor. I slowly got up, thinking my plans through, as I looked around and soon found what I was looking for. Quickly I fell in behind three men who each wore a Gold Ring upon their finger and, wearing my own Gold Ring, I followed them to the council room.

We walked down two long and heavily guarded corridors into another part of the stronghold. At the end of this hall lay the High Council chamber and apparently Zorr himself.

My plan was to enter the chamber and immediately seek to take captive this Zorr, if possible. I would capture this upstart leader and hold him as hostage, so to ensure my escape. If I could do so. At least such was my plan. I knew this action had to be done with the utmost speed and timing, because I was not concealed, and doubtless Zorr—whoever he might be—would not recognize me. He would know I was not Crovis as soon as he saw me.

With my hand on the hilt of my sword I entered the High Council room. The first thing I saw was a large table with many men seated around all sides. These were the powerful and vaulted members of the High Council. Half of these men were dressed in black robes and hoods while some were not. Yet I noticed all prominently wore Gold Rings upon their fingers and all wore face masks. At the far end of the table opposite from me sat the man who was Zorr—still masked and concealed, much to my dismay. I could not identify him.

No sooner had I seen the enemy leader than he raised his right hand in a tight fist. It was obviously some kind of signal. I wondered what it might mean. I was soon to find out. Suddenly from behind me I felt a half dozen sword points pressing into my back. I was immediately told to drop my weapons or die. I sighed; it looked like my game was up. I had been found out.

Helpless and outnumbered I had no choice but to very carefully and slowly drop my sword and dagger to the floor. Then the commander came over to me and grabbing my hand pulled off the Gold Ring that I wore.

"See, Master," he said addressing Zorr triumphantly, "this is the ring of

Crovis! This man is not Crovis, he is a spy, just as I suspected."

Zorr only nodded knowingly. His hideous face showing hatred and rage on the mask he wore. I wondered what his true face looked like underneath that mask, but it looked as though that was information I would never find out now.

Immediately I was roughly tied down to a chair while every man there looked upon me as the enemy I was. All wore masks, but I could imagine their hidden faces showed the exquisite tortures they were imagining for a spy who had infiltrated the very central presence of the headquarters of their lord and master.

The commander of the stronghold walked over to me and threw the Gold Ring at my face. Then he slapped me considerably until Zorr ordered him to stop.

"Insolent barbarian swine!" the commander shouted at me in rage, "but I am sure Zorr has known of your whereabouts ever since you slew Crovis and stole his ring."

Now I smiled. "Ah, then he is not so very wise and all-knowing, as you seem to believe," I said defiantly, adding, "but know that it was not I who killed that worm, Crovis. I was never in Aboola at all. Your intelligence is not as vaulted as you think it to be."

This news made him mad. He suspected I was lying, but I think he knew the truth. The commander struck me harder in the face, he was filled with rage— and I suspect a twinge of fear that he had made some error in his information. Then he suddenly stopped and walked to where the mysterious figure of Zorr was seated. The Master whispered some words to the commander, and then he came back to me. I did not like the look of that sinister stance.

"We believe you did not kill our agent, Crovis," he told me without emotion. "It is of no import however, for Crovis was only a minor agent. If you did not kill him then someone else you know did the deed and that means there is some organized group set against us. We want to know who they are. We want to know your plans and the names of all in your group of conspirators."

"You forget the key factor here," I said arrogantly, "you are the conspirators! The criminals!" For that moment the commander ignored my reply and turned to a different course of reasoning. The man, I thought, was a most effective torturer, quite sadistic, and he had not even begun his work yet.

"For instance, we know who you are," he told me confidently. "Prince Tan Alvaka of Asudra. You are a brave and foolhardy young man but tell us what we wish to know and you shall live. Better yet, you shall have riches and power you cannot imagine. Do not cooperate, and you shall receive the most horrible pain the mind of man can conceive of."

"I think not," I said, remaining bluntly defiant. I would never cooperate with them, but I was disgusted at my capture. I felt that I had failed once again, but I remained defiant and determined. I raised up my bound body as far as I could and spit full into the face of the commander. He was wearing his mask, but the effect was the same as if my spittle had hit his physical face. I could almost see his rage burn through the mask. I could certainly feel it.

I could tell that he grew livid with anger at the insult, and he came for my neck with his hands outstretched to choke the life out of me. I could not move and soon his vise-like grip was upon my throat, pressing hard, cutting off my breathing. I was helplessly at his mercy now and began to squirm and gasp for breath until suddenly I sank into unconsciousness. The last thing I remember before everything went black was a commotion to my side, where I unaccountably thought I saw Droth of all people, with a drawn sword charging at the commander. None of this made any sense to me at the time, it must have been some pre-death fever dream, but soon I drifted into a dark unconscious void.

CHAPTER 6

When I awoke, I found myself laying on a damp stone floor in a completely dark room. It appeared to be some type of jail cell. I was sure that is exactly what it was. I was at least relieved to find that I was apparently still alive, though how long that would last I was not so sure. As my senses came back to me, I became aware that I was unbound, but conscious of someone who was laying on the floor near me.

It was dark in that cell, and it took some time until my eyes got used to the gloomy blackness.

"Who are you?" I asked the man next to me, wondering just where I was. Who was he? And what was to come of me now?

"It is I," the voice said simply. "It is I, Droth."

"Droth?" I replied curiously, soon showing evident surprise. I did recall seeing his image just as I lost consciousness, when the commander had been strangling me. That was a memory I chose to forget. "What are you doing here?"

"I am sorry, my friend," he told me with genuine sorrow. "I am sorry I was unable to come to your aid sooner, but I was being watched."

"Come to my aid? Watched? And you call me *friend?* Why? What is this all about?" I asked wondering exactly what he was trying to tell me. Of all the people I knew in my life, why should Droth come to my aid? He was a captain in this secret society, and a scoundrel and killer. He was no friend to me at all.

"My orders," he told me with a grim leer, and much to my consternation, he said simply, "were to assassinate this Zorr."

"What orders?" I asked confused now.

"Yes, my orders, I will explain."

"You had better," I looked at him in disbelief.

He smiled grimly, then continued, "When you left to attend the High Council, knowing you are not a member of Zorr, I realized that must have been your intention also. So I came to aid you. I could not get there in time, for no sooner did I leave the Great Hall than I was taken prisoner as a spy."

"You? A spy? That is impossible," I told him. "You are a loyal member of this crazed outlaw cult—a killer and a monster."

"No. Not quite so, I am afraid," Droth told me with a slim grin, "because, actually, *I am a spy.*"

I looked at him with a frozen face of shock.

"I do not understand any of what you are telling me, Droth," I told him more confused than ever.

Droth apologized and began to explain to me what he was all about. It was all about a war, and a secret war at that, being fought throughout the world of Rigel.

It seems that this Zorr, and his followers—also known as the secret society of Zorr, as it was called—had become a serious threat to all of the free cities on my world. These Zorrs were more numerous and powerful than ever I realized. They had been laying low and through bribery, threats, key assassinations, manufactured wars, and bloody murder, had taken power in almost every civilized city-state on the planet. They were in complete control in five cities and had powerful agents of influence in about two dozen more cities, including the most powerful city-states of Cathor, Aboola, Asudra, Bovar, Vorba, Bamhor and Daron. Soon this secret society that was nothing more than a blight of hate, slavery and treachery threatened to trample over the freely independent cities of my world and proclaim itself a vast slave empire of Zorr.

It seems to have begun long ago in Cathor, with the ousting of the wicked Sar-Zel and the Zel clan from power. Hotath Zel's ancestors. From then on agents of this man Zorr have worked with only one goal in mind, infiltration of all aspects of life in our free cities, with the eventual total control of our world. It seemed too fantastic to believe that they were now so close to success. The Zels of Cathor, the family from whence Cathor's hereditary rulers have come, fell from favor, and a maddened group of revolutionary leaders came to power. That group was soon overthrown by Kartor's grandfather. Now Kartor still ruled, but he had no heir and he was an old man in ill health. It was said his mind and thinking had gone soft. He would not last long as the leader of the city.

Meanwhile the ousted revolutionaries left Cathor and fled into the Hills of Mystery where there were half a dozen internecine criminal bands. Soon they degenerated into mere assassins, thieves and outlaws. Then one day a man known only as Zorr came in among them. No one knew who he was, or where he was from, but he quickly united all the outlaw bands, organized them, and gave them purpose. Now they have a highly efficient undercover spy network with agents in all the civilized cities.

This history lesson told to me by Droth was all well and good, but I wanted to know where Droth fit in. Until this moment I had thought he was a loyal servant of Zorr—an outlaw and enemy. Also, why if he was against these Zorrs as he proclaimed, why had he tortured me? So now he claimed to be on my side? I had many questions. This was hard for me to believe. It did not seem to make any sense or fit in with the character of that same cruel Droth I had met that day not so long ago upon the plains near Cathor.

Then Droth told me the rest of his story. He spoke allowing a sly smile. "Not long ago a group arose among the Zels of Cathor. They had guessed the truth about the cult of Zorr, though none of them had thought this far in detail about how powerful the enemy had become. They set up an underground organization to combat the warriors of Zorr. It was a small group, insular and secret as it had to be, but efficient. It worked well until the Zels were found out and exiled from Cathor as criminals and conspirators by the emperor. The emperor was an old man and easily controlled and badly advised by his corrupt ministers."

I nodded, I knew most of the history, but not this aspect of it.

Droth told me, "The goal of the Zorrs is complete control and enslavement of the entire world of Rigel, and they have killed untold thousands already in their secret war and terrorized many cities into submission. There is one secret group working against them. They are the Togs, their sworn enemy. The goal of the Togs was to create a secret group pledged to stop the Society of Zorr at any cost. I am of that group, Tan."

I looked at the big nomad chieftain in wonder and surprise. I had never guessed the truth—if in fact this was the truth. After all, Droth had tortured me and tried to kill me, so I believed that some explanation was in order, and I told him so.

"To be such an agent, to play such a deadly game, one must change his ways and the things he does, even if it disgusts him at times," Droth told me, and I could see the pain in his face that this brutal admission caused him. "When I first met you Prince Tan, I thought you were truly a Zorr, and a Gold Ring wearer at that. Very important. Therefore I tried to have you killed, for you were an enemy and gave me none of the secret signs of the Tog Brotherhood. But you did not act like a true Zorrr leader either because you ran away from us, who were supposedly your own comrades. This perplexed me and I was puzzled by your actions. Then one of my men noticed your Gold Ring and we quickly revived you. I would have, at this stage, seen to your death—to give you a gentle push over into dark oblivion. However, I had a mission to kill Zorr and I could not add suspicion to myself by killing one of his high-level agents. I had to maintain the fiction. I am sorry."

"I see that now," I told him, accepting his apology. "You were in a difficult position."

"Most difficult, my friend. Your presence caused me no little amount of concern and consternation. My men surely would have spoken up—with swords mostly likely—for each one of them yearned for my captain's rank. Assassination of commanders is one way to move up in rank among the Zorrs. So I decided to put on an act, asking pity as any normal and cowardly Zorr would do. I may have overdone it, but… In any case, when you granted me pity, I knew there was indeed something strange about you and later realized you were not a Zorr at all. I was most concerned by this and intrigued. For I also knew you were certainly not a member of the Togs."

"Quite a conundrum. I seem to have caused you much concern," I told him with a slight smile.

"Most bothersome, let me tell you," Droth admitted with a light grin. "I quickly realized that whoever you were, you were dangerous and needed watching. Even in our small group of the Togs, we have spies and informers—and it is far worse among the Zorrs. I myself am known only to one man in the Tog group, and he was reported captured and slain. He was a brave warrior, who had killed that fiend Crovis of Aboola."

"Killed Crovis? Not Hotath Zel!" I blurted truly surprised to hear this.

"Yes, that was his name."

"Well, my friend, Hotath Zel is not dead! He is just as alive as you or I, at least he was the last time I saw him—when he slew that fiend Crovis. He is the one who gave me the Gold Ring he took from the corpse of Crovis."

At the sound of these words Droth looked at me amazed. He was visibly shaken, "You know Hotath Zel?"

"Of course," I told him. "It was Hotath who sent me to Cathor to warn his family and try to kill the leader of this cult, if I could do so. Too bad I never made it to Cathor. I can not believe he is dead. It can not be true."

"Indeed, my brother was truly a great warrior and I shall not fail to avenge his murder," Droth said with considerable control in his voice.

"Your *brother*? Truly?" I asked in astonishment.

"Yes, the man who I had thought of merely as Droth replied sadly. "It was Hotath who formed the Togs long ago, and now the underground and resistance shall suffer much because of his death. A great loss to us all, and to Rigel."

"I can not believe he is dead," I told Droth firmly. "When I left him, he was alive and well."

"Then we shall see," he added without emotion. "I hope you are correct, Prince Tan Alvalka."

That night in our prison cell, the man I now knew as Droth Zel and I talked much. I found him—the true man that he was—to be much like his brother and nothing like the cruel and evil captain he had professed to be. He had merely been playing a part. A terrible part to be sure.

"That is all over with now," Droth told me with a sigh, allowing his utter relief to show. "We have been found out and shall soon die by some exquisite torture, I am sure. If you think the torture you received out on the plains that day was bad—and I am sorry about the use of those nasty *xos*—but at the time I did believe you to be an enemy Gold Ring—so it was nothing less than you deserved. Regardless, that will be nothing as compared to what those expertly trained in pain here can do. The Zorrs excel in the torturing arts, they could have written the proverbial book on the subject."

Both Droth Zel and I were now held in a small, damp cell that was completely dark. It was deep and tall. We were still unbound. Only one thin sliver of light filtered in from far above so that we knew we were in a cell that had to have walls very high in height. At the top was a door that seemed to open onto the floor of the lowest corridor of this massive structure. I had no doubt it was guarded. However, guards or not, it did not matter for us since there was no way we could get up there to reach any exit.

"If I am not mistaken," Droth told me almost automatically, "no man has ever come out of this cell alive. It is like a tomb. They call this place The Pit of Death."

That did not sound encouraging to me. I asked my companion, "Why don't they just kill us?"

"Ah, the ways of the Zorrs are most mysterious, but they enjoy their nasty games."

"Torture?" I asked.

"Yes, and worse…"

I wondered what Droth meant by that—something worse than death! It was an ominous statement and he did not want to elaborate on it. I knew that in any case, we were soon to find out.

I just shook my head, "We are getting out of here, I promise you! Somehow, we are getting out of here!"

Droth just looked at me and allowed a grim laugh, not at anything particularly funny, but at our helpless predicament. It was all he could do to keep up our spirits for the moment.

"Just to cheer me up a bit," I asked with a tight-lipped look. "Tell me, how many of them did you kill when you burst in on the High Council? I saw a glimpse of your blade blazing like a whirlwind, but I missed it all when I went unconscious. I hope you got that commander."

"Quite a few met their deaths."

"And the commander?" I asked hopefully.

Droth Zel sadly shook his head in the negative.

I muttered a sigh, for I would have liked to see that arrogant monster taken down. There was not much left to us at that point, so we both settled down to get some much needed sleep.

CHAPTER 7

Droth and I were both exhausted, so we slept for some hours. We did not know how long. When I awoke my face was wet and I felt myself sitting in a low puddle of water. What was this? I was surprised and curious. I wondered what was going on. I soon discovered that water was falling at a thin but steady stream from above us and it was the spray from it that awoke me. Droth had also noticed it. Soon water was coming down at a faster rate so that in about sixty *ban* I feared it would be over our heads. That got our attention. Soon the water was up to our knees and still rising!

"Do they intend to drown us?" I asked with some surprise.

"Most probably," Droth replied with a grim leer.

"I would have expected better of them."

"I as well."

The water was rushing down from above, from the top of the cell some one hundred *haad* above, and there was no way we could get up there to stop it. Or get out of that cell. I realized that we were not just in a regular jail cell, but it surely was some kind of torture cell. The water just kept pouring in steadily as we tried to hold down our panic. There was nothing we could do about it. Eventually the water was up to our necks. Soon it would be over our heads. We tried to climb the walls but they were too slick and we could not get any kind of hold to raise ourselves upwards, even when I hoisted Droth upwards on my shoulders.

Then suddenly the water stopped. It had reached up to our chins. Suddenly the door a hundred *haads* above us opened emitting the first light we had seen in two *talas*. The sudden illumination burned our eyes and it took some time getting used to. I looked up, but could make out nothing.

"Wonder what they're going to do now?" I asked with growing concern.

"They better do something fast to get us out of here!" Droth answered, a hint of frantic fear in his voice. "I can not swim."

"I do not think they intend to save us from drowning," I told my friend in a glum tone.

"You are probably correct, Tan," Droth spoke up suddenly with a wry grin.

Then a surreal voice spoke down to us from above in a malign tone. "Well now, prisoners, you need not worry. Droth Zel, you will not need to swim to save your miserable life, but you shall need these."

We were wondering what the voice was talking about.

Suddenly two slim daggers were thrown down to us.

"What is this?" Droth asked as we each picked up one of the daggers.

"You shall need them," the voice advised us from above. "You see, I have a plan for you both, and the fun is just beginning."

That was an ominous threat but at least it felt good to hold a weapon in my hand again, even if it was just a dagger. Droth also felt the same way I did, for now I saw the determined grin upon his face with him having access to a weapon.

"You will be interested to know," the voice from above continued in his taunting tone, "that Aboola is once again under our complete control. And Prince Tan, Asudra is leaning our way, soon to be conquered completely!"

"Get us out of here!" I shouted in anger.

Our tormentor just laughed and soon the door above was slammed shut.

Droth and I were once again shrouded in darkness, with the water up to our necks. While the water was still there, lapping at our necks, at least now we had a dagger. Why they had been given to us I could not fathom. Having a weapon can give one a sense of hope in such a tight situation. I just wondered what was next, for I could not believe that this was all that would be set against us.

I was not wrong. For soon afterwards the door above was opened once more and a dozen or so, of what looked to be small sea creatures—of all things— were thrown down into our cell. They swam around in the cell and all around us. Why these sea creatures? I could not figure it out until Droth let out a yell of excruciating pain, followed by a lusty curse.

"*Cragas*!" Droth yelled out in warning. "Hurry, my friend, we must kill them before they eat us alive!"

"They are only small ocean things and there are only a few of them," I said, for being a landsman I had never seen these sea animals before.

"They are deadly and they will eat us, tear us apart, small piece by small piece. They are ravenous and never stop eating"

Now I realized the danger was more serious than I first thought, and we began slashing the beasts with our daggers as we received numerous small bites from the beastly creatures. They were small but ferocious and their bites were extremely painful.

The *craga* is double the length of an adult man's hand and they have not one—but three rows of razor sharp teeth. There were about a dozen of them unleashed into our cell and they could literally tear us to pieces unless we killed them first. Soon we each were torn and cut from a dozen vicious bites. However, no matter how furiously Droth and I slashed at them—they were amazingly quick!—we were soon both bleeding from dozens of small vicious bites before I had finally killed the last of the deadly *cragas*.

No sooner had I killed that last *craga* than the water was drained out of our cell from a small opening at our feet. The cell was draining out the water quickly now. Soon the water, which had been a deep red with a mixture of our blood and *craga* blood, was gone and we could see the small drain opening at our feet. It was perhaps the width of a man's hand in diameter, way too small for our use to escape from the cell. But at least the water was now gone. Now I wondered what was next.

Exhausted from our ordeal Droth and I sank down to the floor when I noticed something small moving up through the small hole at my feet.

"Now what!" Droth gasped.

"*Xos*!" I told my companion in shock and terror, recalling my earlier involvement with them. "Look, they're crawling upwards through the drain at our feet."

"We must block it. We cannot allow them to get in here!"

I nodded, but how? We took what clothing we had to stuff up the hole, but it did not work for long. The little horrible creatures were most persistent—especially when they sensed food. Which was us!

Now there were dozens of the horrible insect horrors in the cell grabbing onto our legs with long pincers and biting us furiously as we fought like demons to kill them. We still had our daggers and that helped, but it was hard work—the little demons were very fast. Soon both my legs, as well as Droth's limbs were numb from the paralyzing venom injected from their bites through their teeth. No matter how many of them we killed, more came into our cell through the drainage hole below.

Quickly I grabbed what clothing we had, as well as handfuls of dead *xo* bodies of the fiends we had already killed, and frantically stuffed them all into the drainage hole. Droth brought over more dead insect bodies and we worked feverishly to stuff them down into the drain. Soon we had it clogged up fairly well. Our plan worked! Now no more of the vicious insects could enter our cell, and it was easier for us to dispose of the few remaining creatures that had been able to come at us.

When the *xo* threat was over, we sighed and collapsed for we were both exhausted. For the moment it seemed that our captors had grown bored of their torment of us and soon we fell off to sleep. I do not know how long we slept, but when I awoke I was conscious of something brushing against my face. It shocked me and I instantly grabbed at it. What new terror was this? I lunged for it—at first I thought it was some long coiling snake—but it turned out to be a rope suspended down to us from the open door above. I woke Droth.

"What new deviltry is this?" Droth exclaimed in anger.

"I know not, but we must make use of it to get out of here, if we can," I said quickly. "Come, let us climb up and see where it leads."

Soon the two of us were eagerly climbing upward. To what fate we had no idea—but it was one way out of that cell of horrors and we were all for taking any opportunity for freedom.

"This might be another trick," I warned Droth in a whisper to caution his growing hope, and my own, as we nimbly and quietly climbed the thick rope upwards. We went higher and higher to that opening and towards freedom.

"It may well be a trick, but on the other hand, perhaps one of the secret Togs here has come to our aid?"

I looked at him dubiously but kept hope within me.

We knew that Droth was not the only Tog agent infiltrated against Zorr in this place—there must be others. I nodded, at least I hoped that was the case. I knew that we would find out the truth of this soon enough.

We had gone up roughly 90 *haads* on the rope and had only 10 *haads* more to go when we heard stark laugher from a voice that I instantly recognized as the commander of the stronghold. Then he appeared at the opening. He was still wearing a black robe and hood and wore a hideous mask covering his face, but the man's voice was unmistakable. If I ever discovered who this man might be, I would teach him a lesson for everything that he had done to terrorize us.

"You are correct, Tan Alvaka," the man told me, the mask covering his face contorted with evil pleasure at our plight. We had fallen for another trick. I cursed their foul games. "Yes, this is another of my little games. I hope you enjoy it."

Then as Droth and I quickly struggled upwards to get out of the cell—and at his throat!—I saw the man draw a golden dagger and quickly cut into the rope.

Instantly the rope split and Droth and I plummeted down to hit the floor of the cell below with a hard thump, all bruises and pain. We felt like fools for falling for such an obvious trick.

We were both shaken up from the fall but otherwise the major harm was to our pride for falling for another insidious trick, and yet we both realized now that the only way out of the death cell was by somehow reaching that portal above us and climbing through it.

We had not eaten in two days, nor could we bring ourselves to eat the bodies of the *cragas* or *xos* which littered our cell floor and were now giving up a terrible stench.

A few *talas* after the rope had been cut, the commander came once again to the opening apparently to torment us once more. He suddenly threw down a cloth bag containing a tin of water and a few *osk* legs of meat.

"You have put on a most amusing show," he told us laughing with his usual cruelty, "so I have decided to reward you both. Here is some food and drink. Enjoy it, it may be your last."

We eagerly opened the bag and grabbed the meat and tin of water and prepared to devour it all. We noticed that our sadistic captor was looking down at us with an evil leer and intense interest.

Before Droth and I sampled any of this surprising gift, we froze and looked at each other most thoughtfully.

"One thing I feel I must warn you about however," the voice from above told us trying to repress his laughter. "The food—of course—may be poisoned."

Then the man let out a mockingly uncanny laugh. We could hear him even when he had closed the door above and walked away from the cell. Once again we found ourselves in total darkness. Starving, but with food—*but did we dare eat it?*

Droth and I looked at each other carefully, the gnawing pangs of hunger were clawing at our insides. We were starving men—with food in our hands. I could smell that slavering aroma of the roasted *osk* leg. It was intoxicating, but dare we eat it? We had been told it was poisoned. Or was it? That it was just another cruel joke from our tormentor we were certain. But *was* it poisoned? What should we do?

"I do not think we should eat it, not yet," Droth said thoughtfully, "but it could be useful, if ever we decide to commit suicide."

"Sorry, I will never take that road, my friend," I told him firmly. I looked at the food. It was there before us, calling out to us to eat it. "I think this poison is another cruel ruse. I am betting that if we eat this food, we shall not die. After all, they do not want to kill us in such a manner. At least, I do not think so."

"You take a dangerous gamble, my friend,"

"Perhaps, but this is what they want—to terrorize us—not to kill us," I told him with a smile. "At least not yet."

Droth just shook his head. I wondered if he was giving in. Making plans for suicide did not go over well with me. We had been through much together and it had taken it's toll on our minds and thoughts. We were in a desperate and apparently hopeless situation. To me it seemed that Droth was close to the point where he would welcome death, and the problem of the poisoned food, made our situation worse. I was not far behind him in that regard, but I wondered boldly, was the food truly poisoned? Might that just be another cruel ruse by the Commander? It was surely in keeping with his sadistic nature.

I still hoped for some plan where we could escape from this apparently unreachable pit of a cell. We had to escape but there seemed no way to do so. For now we tried to ignore the food and slept. And waited.

How long we slept I did not know, nor did I know how long we had been imprisoned in that horrid pit of the dead, but when we awoke I noticed that once again, like the time before, a rope had been suspended far down to us. The thick rope hung just over our heads and seemed to be leading to freedom once more.

"No! I will not fall for that trick again!" Droth shouted at me when I stood up to reach the rope. "I will not go up there again to partake in that cruel monster's game! Tan, our tormentor will just cut the rope when you get near the top."

I nodded in agreement, but I was not giving up. I also thought the same thing as Droth, but as I saw the extended rope and the open portal above, I knew that I had to try it. Any chance of escape was better than just standing there and remaining a prisoner. Freedom was so close, yet seemed so distant.

Finally another masked warrior in a black hood and robe came to the opening. It did not seem to be the commander this time. His body size and

"YOU TAKE A DANGEROUS GAMBLE, MY FRIEND."

movements were different. I wondered who this fellow might be, and what his game might be? Something cruel and terrible I was sure.

"What is wrong with you two! Quickly now," he whispered impatiently, "we have no time, you must escape now! Climb the rope to freedom. Hurry now! What is taking you so long? Why do you not come up?"

"Certainly," Droth laughed most bitterly, "we'll be up as soon as I wash and bathe myself, and put on fresh clothing! Go tell the commander we are not playing any more of his sick games!" Then my companion laughed in rage at what he thought was the commander's feeble ruse.

"What are you talking about? Are you mad? You must hurry!" the man above implored us more impatient now then ever. "What nonsense are you talking about. Now hurry! Climb the rope!"

Droth laughed at the man's impatience, saying angrily, "I am not falling for that ruse again!"

Then it suddenly came to me that this was no ruse at all by the commander. Just maybe this man was an agent of the Togs who had come here to save us. Could it be a rescue? There certainly were some Togs in this stronghold. Secret agents. Or so I thought.

Quickly I realized that our weakness from hunger and paranoia was doing just what the commander wanted, we were staying prisoners of our own volition! The very though shocked me into action.

Quickly I motioned for Droth to follow me as I climbed the rope. We were weak but rested after our sleep but we struggled to raise ourselves to just underneath the opening. It was not far now. Droth feared the commander coming back again cutting the rope because we were so close to getting free from of the Death Pit.

I painfully climbed up the last part of the rope. Soon I reached the warrior's hand that he extended to me, and I was pulled up out of the Pit of the Dead. Once free from the pit we both took a hold of Droth and lifted him up and out also.

Glorious liberation!

We were out of that damnable cell now. Droth and I were so thankful and could not believe our good fortune. The warrior was the only person we could see in the corridor. In truth he must be one of the secret agents of the Tog movement.

"I am sorry that I could not get here sooner. I have just heard what happened with you," the warrior told us, "but what took you so long to climb up the rope?"

When we told him all about what had occurred he also grew disgusted by our sadistic treatment, but he was not surprised by it, knowing the commander.

"It will do you no good to get your revenge against him now," he told us quickly. "The commander is no longer here. He is leading the warriors in the siege of Vorba. It is said the city will soon fall. You both must escape now while you have the chance. Here, I have swords, masks, and black robes for you both."

Droth and I quickly donned these and now armed and free, the warrior led us into more winding corridors of the immense stronghold. We went down the last corridor and it was here the warrior left us to our own devices.

"I must leave you now."

"We thank you for your help."

The warrior just nodded.

"What is your name?" I asked grateful for his aid.

"Do not ask my name, I am just glad that I could be of service to you," he told us with a grim smile.

We shook hands heartily and then he was gone.

Now Droth and I were left alone in a long winding corridor as we proceeded to find our way to the stables so as to obtain two good mounts and get away from this place.

Eventually we reached the stables and gave the attendant a phony story and soon we were walking down a large ramp leading our two ponderous mounts. Here we came to another corridor, the end of which led to the Southern Portal and freedom. Four guards stood there menacingly as we approached the exit.

"What is your business?" the leader of the group demanded of us.

I looked at Droth carefully. We thought of fighting our way out of there, for there were only four of them, and we were now armed with swords. However, I noticed that behind these men was another large group of warriors coming towards us leading their mounts. It would be stupid to fight for we would be vastly outnumbered, and even if we were able to ride away, we would be pursued and recaptured as soon as we attempted to escape. Soon this other group of about 40 warriors was closer behind us.

"Well?" the guard leader demanded of us. "Are you deaf or dumb? Do you have any orders or a pass to leave the stronghold?"

The other group was right behind us now and their leader growing annoyed at the wait to be allowed to leave their fortress stronghold.

"Hurry it up!" a voice behind me shouted. "We must leave immediately. We are already late. Mighty Zorr will have our skins!"

"I'm waiting! You two, what is your mission?" The guard leader asked Droth and myself. "Orders! Give me good reason or I shall imprison you for desertion."

"Desertion? You are daft!" Droth told the guard.

Just then an officer from behind me came towards us.

"What is going on here?" In a loud authoritative voice he demanded, "My men and I are late as it is. Why are you guards holding us up?"

"It is these two, sir," the guard replied carefully. "They have no pass nor any papers, no reason to leave."

"We have become separated from our group," I said offering up the best excuse I could think of at the moment. "They left this morning for Vorba."

I had told them the only reason that came to my mind and by the look upon their faces, luckily it had been the correct thing to say that made sense to them.

"There, Sergeant," the officer of the larger group of warriors told the guard leader, "they shall ride with us to Vorba. I can always use extra men in my unit."

"Thank you, Captain," I said with a salute.

"You and your fellow, get in line and come with us," the Captain ordered us and we obediently fell into line, leading our mounts among his group of warriors. We fell in at the end of the group.

Quickly without further words Droth and I followed the officer as the portal was opened. Then we mounted our huge *zibas* and rode out of the enemy stronghold and out to freedom.

Freedom of a sort.

We were now a part of Tabak's group and on our way south to aid in the conquest of Vorba. Both Droth and I knew we had to get away from this group soon. As Tabak's men rode through the long winding mountain road we gradually urged our mounts to fall back until we were the last riders in line. Then seeing a good opportunity for escape when the group had turned a bend, we quickly rode off the road and into the thick underbrush.

We were now separated from Tabak's group and surrounded by high, full trees that obscured us very well. We became very cautious now, looking upwards for guards that might be posted in the trees or upon the cliffs of the hills. It was while we were looking to our left side that we were hailed by a voice from over at the right. What was this? Who was this, I wondered?

Droth looked at me carefully, his hand moving to the hilt of his sword.

We did not have long to wait. Instantly from behind a large outcropping of rock six warriors approached us with drawn swords. They looked serious and I could see they meant their business.

"We have been watching you," one of them said slyly, "and we seem to notice that you are not following your group. Stragglers or deserters."

"Yes," I admitted readily, for their was no sense to lie about that—I would have more important things to lie about soon. "We have become lost and cannot find them. We are new recruits and were on our way with Tabak."

"I know Tabak," one of them said.

They came closer and then told us to dismount our *zibas*.

"Dismount? Why?" Droth asked the one who was apparently their leader, his hand still upon the hilt of his sword. We were both ready for battle, but with the odds of six to two I thought it better to try to talk our way out of this, if possible.

"This is why, Droth!" one of the six said with a growl. Now we realized that they recognized us and all six of them quickly drew their weapons and charged at us.

It seems they knew Droth and I had escaped from their stronghold and I realized that their leader had been one of Droth's men, when I had first come upon his group in the desert. We had made a colossal mistake. We drew our swords and quickly jumped upon our mounts and met the six as they turned to come at us.

We fought a wild fight, flashing swords and ringing metal, but I soon realized that these six men were not good swordsmen, nor were they the best of riders. Droth and I were able to ride around them as our swords cut through their guard and did them much damage. It seems these men were more used to killing defenseless women and children than armed and trained warriors. It was not long before three of our attackers went down, and at that point the other three fled, riding away as quickly as they could into the woods. However, before they could reach the tree line, Droth and I brought down one more of our attackers.

Two of them had gotten away. It was their leader, and another, and we had to make haste before they brought reinforcements to come after us.

Like lightning we raced through the woods and soon a little while later we were out of the Hills of Mystery and onto the plains below. No sign of pursuit had followed us as yet and I sighed with relief as we rode on.

"One of us must go to Cathor," Droth told me in a firm tone. "We need to get our troops collected to help the defense of Vorba. That someone is you, Tan. I may not go because the Zel clan is outlawed there, as you know."

I nodded in agreement. So it was decided I should ride to Cathor. Meanwhile Droth would go to Vorba and do his best to help the defenders until I returned with an army of Cathor troops to break the siege and end the conquest. We then said our good byes and spilt up going our own way; I to the south, and he to the southeast.

That night a lay alone, camping out by a protective grouping of huge boulders. After a large dinner of *squal* meat and edible bitter leaves, I relaxed. The *squal* was good and tastey, a small rodent-like creature that is plentiful on the plains. They make a decent meal when cooked in a low fire. They are plentiful upon the plains and I was easily able to catch one for my meal. It tasted extremely good. I was lucky to have captured one of the quick little beasts for my evening meal. Then well fed, I wrapped myself in my blanket and was soon asleep.

The next morning I was up early riding my trustworthy *ziba* hard and fast south towards Cathor. I was lucky that I had not run into any other riders or wagons all day. By late afternoon I could see the gleaming, jewel-encrusted spires and towers of Cathor glittering in the distance. Cathor well deserved the title 'the Glittering City of Jewels' I realized, and I quickened my pace to the gate of the beautiful city.

CHAPTER 8

The large heavily guarded main gate into Cathor loomed ahead of me as I rode steadily towards the city. Cathor is a brilliant glittering city of gold domes and high towers. It's people are fabulously rich and successful. It is one of the most powerful city-states upon the world of Rigel, and the only city more powerful than my native city of Asudra.

As I dismounted and walked my mount up to the main gate I was stopped and questioned by a member of the City Guard. I gave the man the story that I was a mercenary from Asudra seeking employment and was soon allowed into the city. It seemed they were in need of as many good warriors as they could get for their army.

Once in the city, walking the wide and expansive streets, my large *ziba* walking silently behind me, I noticed the sheer beauty of Cathor. The architecture of the buildings was impressive and built on a grand scale. Even, one might say, glorious. Everywhere were beautiful straight-lined buildings with high towers and needle-like spires. Sparkling clean streets led to all quarters of Cathor. Everywhere I saw wagons, mounted men, pedestrians, hordes of citizens going about their business in this most bustling of cities. Merchants and venders were apparent everywhere, selling everything that one could imagine. There were weapons aplenty, food of every type, warriors, workers, perfumes, richly woven clothing, and the most lovely women.

I noticed the people seemed to be a mixture of all types and a relatively happy lot who enjoyed life in this rich and powerful city. But I noticed that there would soon be little freedom for them—which seemed evident to me and somewhat of a conundrum when mixed with the happiness I saw in this city. For none of them realized the ominous threat posed by the secret cult of Zorr, and the plans that hung over their heads like a bloody blade of doom that was ready to drop upon them all very soon.

For the cult of Zorr sought to take over control of cities not by war, but by nefarious secret and insidious placement of their minions in offices of control. In that way, they did not need an army to take over a city, only a few key and well-placed officials to make the proper rules and edicts in their direction. It was treason and a form of warfare I had never known before. It gave me much to think about.

I soon reached the central forum or marketplace of Cathor. I tried to keep a low profile and not draw attention to myself. Everywhere there were buyers and sellers doing a vigorous trade in all manner of goods and services. There were farmers from the outlaying districts selling their surplus produce, and workers and artisans selling their various wares. I noticed warriors and officers testing the strength and durableness of all manner of weapons. There were beautiful ladies from the wealthiest and most powerful houses of Cathor looking over all manner of clothes, silks and furs.

One young lady shone among them all and I could not help but notice that she was flanked on both sides by warrior bodyguards and female servants. She was truly glorious. She had long sun-yellow hair and wore a bright white gown upon her slim figure that was decorated with all manner of precious stones. She was truly a marvelous sight to behold. I could not move my eyes away from her lovely form, so much so that soon she caught my stare returning it with a haughty gesture. Then she raised her head to turn her face away angrily. I smiled at that and wondered who she might be, but I decided to put thoughts of her from my mind for the moment. I had an important duty to perform that could not wait.

Suddenly I was distracted by the noise of a large wagon being driven down the street in the opposite direction of the lovely lady. I noticed that it was heavily loaded—overloaded in fact—with huge barrels, most probably of beer or ale. I could see the barrels were shaking and rolling back and forth as the wagon came closer. I could see that the barrels had not been tied down properly, and I knew what that might mean. I looked to the lovely young woman and her retainers, and saw she was walking closer to the wagon oblivious of the threat. Suddenly I heard a loud crash and a rushing rolling sound. Upon turning I saw some of the giant barrels had broken their bonds and were hurling madly down the street knocking people to all sides. These barrels were full of ale and very heavy. They came rolling down the street upon the screaming people like a maddened *ziba* that was out of control.

My eyes quickly moved from the barrels, to the lovely young lady I had noticed earlier. To my horror I saw that she was now directly in the path of the onrushing barrels. She stood in front of them petrified. Her retainers and warriors had all run away to save themselves, leaving her alone. Now she stood there all by herself as the wildly flung barrels crashed madly down upon her. I knew that she could not move out of their way in time, and that certainly one of the barrels would hit her if I did not act. Instantly I ran to her aid. The barrels were rolling furiously down the street closer to her now. There was no way to stop them. I ran, and jumped. I hoped I would be able to make it in time. I saw her standing there alone now, petrified with fear as I ran to her with all the strength the great god Ibar had given me.

While all of this has taken so long to explain, it really happened in an instant, seemingly in the blink of an eye. I was at the young woman immediately within a heartbeat. Soon I was beside her. Then just before the first barrel in the forefront would have hit her, I lifted the young lady aside in my arms to safety. That first barrel flew past my head, crashing into the wall behind us with an explosion of gushing ale—right where we *had* been standing.

A large cheer went up from the populace as they drew closer and I helped the woman to her feet. She was visibly shaken but I admired how she regained her composure so quickly and now held herself in control. She stood up now and cleaned the dirt from her regal clothing as I stood by to offer my assistance.

Now that she was herself again, she came over to me and with a glowing smile and eyes that expressed more than she said, gave me a simple thank you.

"You are welcome, My Lady," I told her, happily that this had all turned out well and that she was unharmed. "I am happy that you are safe. My I have the honor of knowing the name of the lady who it is that I have served?"

"Surely, brave knight," she said regally, but without her former haughtiness at all now, "My name is Dallia, and once again I must thank you for what you did to save me. That was very brave and I was very foolish. I should have moved out of the way but I just do not know…" she stumbled fearful, looked at me carefully. "Everything happened so quickly, before I noticed the accident of the barrels there was nothing I could do. I should have moved, but I was frozen and did not know where to go."

"It is all right. I know how you feel," I told her, marveling at her composure and calmness that had returned so quickly after so harrowing an incident. "I too have been in a position where I have felt hopeless. It is not always that easy to know the right thing to do in every situation."

She smiled at me, and that smile was worth any danger I had been placed in.

I did not mention about my being imprisoned in that death cell in the enemy stronghold in the Hills of Mystery.

We both stood there looking at each other when from out of the crowd a group of Cathor warriors came towards us walking most stridently. A captain of the guard stepped up to us and told Dallia that she was wanted home by her father immediately.

"No! I will not go!" she told the officer in a calm but defiant tone.

"You are coming whether you want to or not. We have our orders. Your father has ordered you to come with us. You are to be at his side at the feast tonight," the captain told her firmly. "Please do not make me force you to obey."

"No!" she barked back just as firmly, then she turned her back to the officer and faced me.

Before she or I could say a word to each other, her arm was grasped and she was suddenly jerked back by the captain. Then he began to unceremoniously drag her away with him.

I was astonished and then enraged by this behavior and could not allow such roughness to a lady. The lady's guards and female servants had all gone. Now she was alone with me and the captain and his men. I grew angry at this treatment of the young lady. I would not allow this to happen, not even if it was the will of the Great God Ibar himself who demanded this girl's attention.

"I think not, captain. I will not allow this, not here and not now!" I growled and moved forward and seized the captain by the throat and hurled him roughly to the ground. "Now be gone, before I lose my patience with you!"

"How dare you! You know who I am!" he shouted in rage.

"You should have better manners with a lady!" I told him with grim purpose, my hand ready to withdraw my sword should the need arise.

The guard captain saw my action and he slowly got to his feet. I fear I was a bit more rough with him that I thought.

"Thank you," the Lady Dallia told me in a soft voice, the luster of her soft blue eyes made it all worth it. To see the approval in her eyes surely warmed my heart. "That is twice you have saved me from a most undesirable situation. Are you some guardian sent to me by the gods?"

I just laughed lightly, "No, My Lady, at least I think not—but I would surely protect you, should you ever have need of my services."

She smiled rather shyly, "What is your name?"

"I am Tan Alvaka, a warrior from Asudra," I told her, not wishing to reveal my royal status as a prince of that noble house.

Just then the guard captain, his pride seriously damaged, stood up and faced me. He mumbled a few oaths and then drew his sword and came at me with murder in his eyes.

I made sure that Dallia was out of danger, then I raised my weapon and stood ready to meet his charge with my sword blade. I did not want to get into a fight with the man, but I had no choice now. The Fate's had decided the matter for me.

The captain's first sword blow was a well aimed lunge that drew quite a bit of blood from my left shoulder. He had struck me by surprise and the strength of his attack had caught me unawares. It would not happen again. Instantly I knew I was facing no slacker with a sword. The man might have been an arrogant bully and a fool but as far as his swordsmanship was concerned, he was very good indeed. I knew he would give me a good run for my money. I parried his next thrust and pushed him away from me. I would also give a good account of myself.

Then he came at me again, harder. Sensing his intent I blocked his thrust and in a quick and sudden swipe gave him a nice slash across his right cheek. There was a thin trickle of blood running down his face now. He would remember that cut, and have evidence of it, for the rest of his life. The blood flowed down his face, and everyone on the street moved back sensing this would now end up in a death duel.

My cut infuriated the man, but I did not care. If he did not back off, I would send him down to the gods of the underworld unto death. I told him so, and that only seemed to enrage him more. However, the captain was a well trained fighting man and quickly tamped down his rage and anger for he knew I was his match, or better, with a sword. He quickly became calm and steady as he came at me again most workmanlike, this time methodical and eager. He was an excellent swordsman and kept me quite busy. He knew most of my tricks, and I knew most of his, so that after the first moments we began fighting furiously back and forth along the street. His men stood around cheering him eagerly, but as yet had not joined in on the fight. For that I was content, but if necessary I would deal with them all too—as best I could.

The fight went on with furious hacking and clashing blades. Thrusts and parries, cuts and swaths of clanging metal sharp as a razor edge. He was fast, but I was just as quick. Each of us pushed for an opening to get at the other. Both of us had received a couple of slight cuts, but nothing of any real danger yet. Neither of us could attain a good advantage upon the other, and although we were both bleeding from a couple of minor wounds, still none were serious enough to impair either of our fighting abilities.

We continued to battle ever more furiously all along the street and in front of stalls and shops. The crowd seemed to be cheering for me, while the nearby Cathor warriors naturally boasted that their captain was just playing with me and that he would soon finish me off. They cheered him, rather unwillingly, it seemed to me. It was obvious that he was not so popular with his men. I was sure that both of us had bitten off more than we could chew so to speak with this encounter, because I think neither of us ever imagined that his opponent would prove to be so good. Indeed it seemed that we were too evenly matched.

It was a hard fought battle, but I would never let him best me.

Slowly but surely I could see that my opponent was working me over to a building and soon I found myself backed up against a brick wall and battling for my life. I could see the worried face of the Lady Dallia in the distance. It gave me strength to see that she was on my side and hoping that I would win this battle. Seeing her so concerned for my safety gave me renewed strength and inspiration, and I fought so furiously that I could see even the Cathor captain become stunned. I fought on ever harder. So did he. Soon he had to fall back from the slashes and lunges of my blade. Now I heard bets being taken as onlookers and guards yelled back and forth who they put their money on to win this sword bout. It seemed to become almost a festive atmosphere, but I knew I was in a fight for my life. Other guardsmen yelled loudly to put down money on their favorite in our battle, almost always their captain, while the merchants of the area bet on my victory.

Then suddenly I was inching my way forward out into the open and away from the wall, when I noticed the captain grab a small board off of a table behind him. Quickly he charged me, keeping my sword busy, and with his other hand he flung the board and hit me square in the face with it. I was knocked down stunned, but I had expected this dishonorable form of attack from him. I saw a triumphant sneer come to his face when he realized I was down, then he rushed forward to finish me off.

Before I was ready to meet him, my eyes caught the Lady Dallia running towards us and suddenly spring upon his back kicking and scratching, giving me enough time to get to my feet and continue the fight. The Lady Dallia fought like a demon but she was unceremoniously thrown off the officer's back as he turned in rage to meet my renewed attack. His face was red with anger and some fear, but he was not nearly as furious as I was myself, and I came at him hard and fast. Never had I fought so well. Nothing could stop my blade now from weaving in and out of his guard. Within moments I had him bleeding from a dozen cuts and soon disarmed him. I left him standing there unarmed and ashamed, I did not want to kill him.

"Submit!" I demanded.

The man nodded reluctantly, rubbing his bruised arm.

Instantly I walked to the Lady Dallia's side to help her up.

"Are you all right, My Lady?" I asked softly, unable to ignore her stunning beauty as my eyes took in her lovely radiance. "You should not have helped me, you put yourself in danger, but I thank you for it."

"I feared you needed the help," she said with a sly grin.

I nodded with a slight smile and walked closer towards her. No sooner had I stood before Dallia than the guard captain shouted out an order and his men rushed forward to surround me.

"Take him!" the guard captain shouted to his men.

I instantly found myself facing a dozen Cathor guardsmen, and I only hoped their swordsmanship was not the equal of that of their captain. If so, I would be in a lot of trouble, but fortunately none of them were that good. As it turned out only two of them were decent swordsmen, and none of them were very brave. Brave only when subduing helpless women and children, I imagined. The usual city guard type.

After their initial charge against me, three of the Cathors lay dead in the street and another was seriously wounded. I no longer had the luxury of granting mercy to my attackers. This was now a battle to the death for me. The guard captain, now armed again, stood back this time, giving his men orders and telling them the best way to take me down. The people were now booing and cursing the cowardice of the captain and his men, but I fought on and quickly another guardsman lay dead in the street. I was not giving up, and I knew that if I did, these men were not going to arrest me—I knew now they were out to kill me!

I found myself once again boxed in against a wall, due to their superior numbers. There were still six of them left, as well as their captain who stood off, safe for now. With my back against the wall I fought all the harder. I also had an advantage since they could not outflank me, nor attack me from behind with the wall at my back. This knowledge gave me added fury and soon two more of my enemy went down, cut hard and deep by the power of my uncanny blade. Now I only faced four very hesitant and not very good swordsmen, who had learned to fear the dreadful death-dealing of my flashing sword. None of them were eager about pressing the attack at all, each one of them more than willing to allow that honor to fall to the man beside him and not himself. I was holding them off rather easily. Soon I would surprise them with a rapid attack, which I knew they were not ready for. Then I spied another group of Cathor warriors coming towards me from another street. I sighed, but fought on. To victory or to death!

I was ready to give up my life if need be and take as many of my attackers with me down to the underworld as I was able. For I knew the end for me was on the way—as this new large group of warriors came closer. I could see now that there were fully a hundred of them!

I saw my one chance and dropped more of the captain's men as shocked reinforcements and citizens looked on. I knew I had to work fast. The remaining guards I quickly disarmed before the new group arrived. I found myself momentarily free surrounded by dead guards, and crying wounded. The reinforcements for the guards approached me very warily and slowly. They got within a dozen *haad* of me when they suddenly stopped, and their commander ordered his men to sheath their swords. I was unable to comprehend the reason for this action but I nodded and in respect, sheathed my own sword as well. I waited. I would not gain anything now by losing my life fighting all these warriors. I still had a mission, and remonstrated against myself for having temporarily forgotten it. I doubted now if anyone in this city would listen to my plea for peace after I had killed nearly a dozen Cathor city guardsmen.

"What's the trouble here?" the new commander asked, looking firmly at the captain. "We had the report of a riot in this section of the city."

"It is that man over there," the captain said pointing at me with intense fury and hatred. "He has killed my men!"

The Commander turned towards me with a puzzled look. He eyed me carefully. "How many men do you have with you? Where are your men?"

"I am the only one, I am here by myself," I replied grimly. I saw the Lady Dallia come over to see what was happening and looked very sad at my fate. Her own bodyguards and female servants, who had now returned since it was safe, led her away. I watched her leave with a heavy heart. Would I ever see her again?

However, I had more pressing matters to deal with now.

"Can this be? You are the one responsible for all this? One man, only you?" the commander asked curiously, then understanding the truth, he looked at the captain and shouted, "You have called me here for a lone warrior you could not deal with by yourself? You damnable coward!"

"He is dangerous!" the captain cried out in rage trying his best to defend his soiled honor. His eyes narrowed upon me with a vile hatred and rage, "This man should be killed immediately. He is dangerous. This one man is responsible for all the mayhem and death you see here, he must be killed. Allow me to do it now, commander!"

"No, you shall not!"

The commander looked at everything around him and seemed to think most carefully. I saw my chance and spoke up.

"Commander, I have an urgent message for the emperor of your city. I am a messenger. Troops must be sent to aid Vorba, before the conquest there is completed by the enemy."

"Fool," the commander told me, "I would not allow you within a spear-length of our emperor, and as for Vorba, special messengers brought the news that the city fell this morning, thank the Great God Ibar."

"Then that is a great tragedy. Why are you so happy that the city has fallen?"

"The city of Vorba has always been our enemy, now we have one less enemy in the world to deal with," the Commander barked with pride.

I shook my head full of sadness.

"WHAT'S GOING ON HERE?"

"Now if you do not come with me willingly," the commander added with a growl, "I assure you, you will not live to fight your way out of this situation. Understand?"

I did, and as they took my sword and dagger from me, my hands were tightly bound and I was escorted under heavy guard down the streets to a large building that I instantly recognized must be the city prison.

CHAPTER 9

The city prison of Cathor is a large multi-storied monstrosity of a building that is ominous looking and heavily guarded. It looked most secure and my hope of escape from such a place seemed to be dashed for now at seeing it. My hands were bound behind my back and I was marched roughly up several levels of the building, and then down various hallways, until I was pushed to a cell inhabited by three other men. I was untied and then unceremoniously thrown to the floor, my guards laughed as they withdrew locking the stout cell door behind them with a loud slam. Here I was in another dire situation.

I stood up and looked around me. I noticed there were three other men in my cell, warriors wearing the fighting insignia and uniforms of the city of Aboola. That was not such good news for me. My city, Asudra, and Aboola, were at war. The cities had been at war for a long time so that we were natural enemies. They eyed me with much curiosity and suspicion.

"What city be your from, stranger?" the biggest one of the three asked me suspiciously. I would later find out that he was known as Beeg. He looked at me curiously, then added, "Your harness is old and worn and you wear no city insignia. You can not be from Aboola."

"No," I told him honestly, there was no use in lying here. "I am originally from Asudra, but I am now a mercenary swordsman. Or I should say, I was until recently. Now I am a prisoner, like you three."

"Not like we three. We are Aboolas."

"We are still all prisoners," I told him.

He and his fellows did not seem to like me reminding them of that.

"So why are you here? What is your crime?" Beeg asked me in a firm tone. It seemed like he was demanding an answer.

So be it, I had nothing to hide. I decided to tell him most of what had happened since I had entered Cathor. So I told them my story. They listened most carefully.

Upon hearing of my battle with the city guard captain, the three men came to life, smiles bursting forth on their dirty, haggard faces. I also noticed in their speech a tone of respect for my prowess with a sword.

"If what you say is true..." Beeg spoke up in a more friendly tone, yet allowing some suspicion, "Well then..."

"It is all true," I replied firmly.

"Then welcome," he told me. "Welcome brother to our prison."

"Thank you, but I would rather it were some other place for me to visit."

"Not just a visit, you are here with us, probably for life—which may not be too long for us," one of the others of the three told me with a grim grin.

I just laughed good naturedly, so be it. I sat down and made myself comfortable in my new home. I decided these three might be good fellows to speak with and to find out about what was going on in the city. With that in mind, the four of us talked for many *tals*. I found the three Aboolas to be friendly and trustworthy once they got over their initial suspicions of me. So much so that I decided to tell them most of what I knew, all about the Zorrs and the Togs and all that I had gone through since I had left Asudra such a long time ago. I also told them about the stronghold in the Hills of Mystery, and the monster who led them known only by the ominous name of Zorr.

My three fellow prisoners, Beeg, Onat and Saad had heard of the Zorrs and when Aboola fell they had fled once they saw the battle was lost. They were determined to continue the fight. So they had come to Cathor, which had been a friendly city, asking for aid, for Cathor was the most powerful city in the world. They would never go to my native city of Asudra because of the war between our two cities. A war by the way created by the Zorrs for their own benefit. Now I surmised that they had created the war for the purpose of weakening both cities—to better conqueror them more easily. This Zorr was a most devious enemy.

I told them all of what the Zorrs had planned and their faces grew grave. Beeg said he never realized that the Zorrs were that powerful. Onat said he had never trusted them. Saad just growled angrily that they had been able to go so far in their conquests and had had so much success.

Time passed, and the more we spoke, we realized we had a lot in common, and we became friendly, knowing we were on the same side in this conflict with the Zorrs. Beeg and myself seemed to have a steadfast goal in defeating the Zorrs in any way possible.

By the next *tala* of my imprisonment I was determined to find some way to escape. We were all in agreement in this action. Yet how my companions and I would accomplish this task, we did not know as yet. It was a dream, but a most forceful one. Our cell was made of brick and very small, and the only way out was through a small metal door that was never opened. All food was thrown in to us through a small opening under the door so that we never even saw our captors and they did not communicate one word to us.

My mind was awhirl with worry and anger at my situation. My mind also kept to itself fearful thoughts concerning the Lady Dallia, wondering if I would ever see her again. It did not seem likely. I admitted freely to myself that I missed her even though I hardly knew her at all. Such are the vagaries of love to one's heart. In any case, it appeared that my life would be short-lived once the powers that be dealt with me. I had killed many city guardsmen, and that tends to make one unpopular with the powers that be. Nevertheless, the Lady Dallia was always close to my thoughts so much so that I was determined more than ever to escape. I also had my duty and mission. I had to find some way to speak with the emperor of the city and alert him to the danger posed by the Zorr cult. Then I had to somehow convince him to take his army and attack the Zorr stronghold in the Mountains of Mystery. With all this done, it would mean the Zorrs would have no base of operations any longer, and each city on the planet would be free from their oppressive yoke and closed off to them.

My prison companions, Beeg, Onat and Saad also agreed with my plan to fight against the Zorr menace so that it was agreed we would escape from this place, and do all we could to make it to the Florian Palace and try to reach the emperor. Whether old Kartor, the emperor of the city, would even listen to our plea was anyone's guess, but we had to at least try to make him see the danger. The people of my world needed to be set free of the Zorr menace.

How I would accomplish our escape—how I would achieve our goal however—was another matter altogether. No matter how many plans we came up with, all seemed doomed to failure if our guard never entered our cell and the door was never opened. It seemed to make any escape impossible.

"We must come up with some idea to get that guard to enter our cell," I told my companions knowing that was the only way for us to escape. Saad came up with the idea of one of us playing sick. When we tried that plan the guard only laughed, saying that we should all get sick and do them the favor—and all die. Then he would not have to come down here twice a day with our meager food ration. So that would not work. We needed another plan.

Our guard was the least charming fellow we had ever encountered, and I say that hiding my great anger towards him, and his foul treatment of us. Beeg wished to met him some day alone when he could rearrange the man's face. I smiled, and told him I hoped that his dream would come true. Then I got more serious and tried to come up with another idea.

"He seems to be a most unpleasant and lazy host," Onat said rather lightheartedly. "We need a new plan, Tan."

I thought about what might work in such a dire situation. It was obvious this guard did not care whether we lived or died. That made things much more difficult for us. Then I came up with something that I did think might work. It was a long shot but it was better than stewing on our haunches and doing nothing. So I got the attention of my companions.

"Suppose," I told them with a sly look, "we give our guard the impression that we are escaping by making all manner of noise? Scraping and banging and whatever. He would certainly be curious. He must. Eventually he will have to enter our cell to check if we are digging our way out."

"I like it," Beeg told me.

"I do not," Saad spoke up, he was in a grumpy mood and I could not blame him.

My other prison companion just shrugged and said nothing. Not a ringing endorsement.

My idea was met with somewhat less than enthusiastic approval by my three companions, but we all admitted it was the only plan we had at the moment, so it was put into motion the next time the guard came around with our food.

In time, we could hear the guard's booted feet shuffling along the stone floor of the prison corridor as he came close to our cell. At that point we began a terible banging and scrapping on the large bricks of our cell. The four of us worked harder and harder using any small piece of metal from our harnesses, scrapping and banging louder and louder and more furious. We were able to create quiet a din.

Eventually our guard came closer and closer so that he could not have missed the noise we were making even if he had been deaf. It was so loud. Our food was thrown into the cell as usual and then, without one word, he left. His footsteps slowly fading into the outer hallways. I was astonished. Saad was angry and disappointed. Nonetheless we were determined that when the guard came around the next time to give us our food we would do the same thing that night. We planned to create such noise that it could not help but attract the attention of any prison guard alerting him to the possibility of our escape.

CHAPTER 10

So later that night, as our guard came around once again, we began our infernal noisemaking, building a racket louder and louder, that no guard could ignore. However still nothing was said by the man and he left the hallway outside our cell without a word. This was most disheartening. That was twice in one day now and our guard had not investigated us about the loud noise we made.

"He must be the most uninterested fellow I have ever encountered," Beeg said with disappointment.

I nodded, "But I will not give up. He must check the reason for the noise sometime. He has to!"

"Must he?" Onat added with a hard look.

"He must be the most dull witted guard there ever was," Beeg replied with a grim laugh.

"No, perhaps he is just plain stupid?" Saad offered, shaking his head.

"More likely, just lazy and he does not care what the sounds might mean," I told them, but I was still determined that our plan had to—*must*—eventually work. So we continued it at every feeding time.

"What is the use?" Onat replied glumly.

"I admit I am getting discouraged, but we must keep this up. It is our only chance for escape I can think of. I admit, I do not understand his reaction— or lack of it—but I will not give up. Not yet. It must be obvious to our guard that we are escaping, or at least trying to do so, but still he does nothing. I do not understand," I stated flatly, feeling rather hopeless that this plan had apparently failed. We had no other plan.

"Perhaps he does not care?" Beeg offered suggestively.

I nodded, "Possible, but would he not be in trouble if we escaped?"

"Who can tell," Onat added with impatience. "You would thnk so, but who can tell."

We kept making our noises of impending escape for two more days without any success. Or no apparent notice by our guard. He did not even shout at us to stop making so much noise. It was uncanny and most vexing. Once the guard did come and just laughed as he passed our cell. That was the only reply he ever made to our efforts. We were all puzzled.

"It must be obvious to this idiot that we are trying to escape," Beeg said, tersely, his voice full of exasperation.

"Of course," Saad added, "the man can not be that dense."

"Suppose we go one step further in our plan?" I asked my companions. They all looked at me expectantly. "Suppose we pretend that we have *already* escaped?"

"That is impossible," Beeg told me.

"Maybe…but he does not know it," I replied with a sly leer.

"Then…?" Saad spoke up curiously.

"Why, then he would have to come into the cell to check up on us!" Onat said with a sly grin.

"Correct!" Beeg told us getting the plan, and we all allowed a knowing smile. "He will have to come into the cell to check on us because he can not see into all areas of our cell clearly, and once he does—he will regret it."

With that plan in mind we quietly awaited for the next feeding time. We stood in the shadows on the same side where the door was located so that even if our guard looked into the cell he could not see us. We were not visible to him. So he would have to actually enter our cell to clearly check on us. But would he? That is what we hoped.

Suddenly off in the distance we heard the footsteps of our guard approaching. This was it! We waited with baited breathe as he came closer and closer, until he was directly at the door to our cell. We did not make a sound. All was dead quiet. The guard came closer and closer to our cell and then near the door. Even when food was thrown into the cell no one spoke or made any sound— no movement—we hardly even breathed.

The guard stopped and tried to look into our cell, but of course he could not see all areas of the cell clearly. He let out a low curse. We could tell that he was puzzled. He looked through the small food slot and tried to view us again, but he could not see us at all. The cell appeared empty to him. That was strange. Now he grew concerned. Suddenly he left the hallway and that seemed to be the last we might see or hear from him until the next feeding time. He seemed to be the most incurious fellow there ever was!

Or so we thought!

Evidently we were wrong about that! For no sooner had our guard left us than we heard his footsteps rapidly approaching once again. Perhaps he had gone to get the key to our cell? I wondered, hoped. All was deathly quiet in our cell. I gave my comrades the signal. This was the moment we were waiting for. Slowly we heard a key enter the lock and turn as our guard cautiously now with sword in hand, warily opened our cell door.

"What have you done? Where are you dirty creatures!" he growled in annoyance.

He was nervous and visibly shaking now, whether from anger at the thought of our presumed escape, or his punishment at not guarding us properly—or because he suspected some trick. I could see the fear upon his face. What the cause of his fear might be I did not know. Nor care. But I could guess. His superiors would not take kindly at any of this—if we had somehow escaped. He would be to blame and severely punished.

Soon our cell door was flung open wide enough to let him pass and he took a reluctant step into our cell. That step was the last one he ever took in this world. For no sooner had his foot touched the floor, then Beeg, Saad, Onat and myself were upon him. He never had a chance!

In an instant Onat disarmed our guard and taking the man's sword he used it to run our guard's own weapon through his heart. Our guard was dead before his body hit the floor.

Now with the avenue to freedom open to us we quietly left our cell and ventured warily into the dimly lit hallway.

We all knew our plan. By any means and as quickly as possible we had to make our way out of this prison and to the Florian Palace to see Kartor, emperor of Cathor. But how to do that? Where was the palace located? I did not know this city. Even if we could reach the palace—how would we get inside? How would we be able to have an audience with the emperor? It seemed impossible, but we did not think about that right then.

I looked at my three companions, "Do you know the location of this building in relation to the Florian Palace?"

We stood alone in the corridor outside our cell, trying to figure which way to go, as none of us was familiar with the layout of this prison. We saw one corridor that led downward, whether to the darkest pits or to the street we did not know, and another corridor perhaps to the roof—or maybe the street level. Again, we did not know.

"The Cathor emperors are most fearful of their enemies—especially assassins," Beeg told me cautiously. "I would bet the Florian Palace is probably on the other side of the city, far away from this prison."

Saad and Onat agreed and soon we decided on that destination.

Then I had another idea. I went back into our jail cell and got dressed in our dead guard's harness and uniform. Then with his sword and dagger, I proceeded to lead my three prisoners through the corridors of the prison. I had found some rope and so bound each of their hands behind their backs— but with slip knots where they could free themselves quickly if necessary. For now they appeared to be my prisoners, and all appeared to be well.

We passed many warriors and guards, but were never questioned. I found a roll of papers and held them meaningfully in my left hand, and whenever anyone looked askance at me and my supposed charges, I said, "Order of the

Commander," and that shut them up.

We made it safely to the street level and I was anxious to leave the prison. Then I heard a sudden loud voice call out from behind me.

"You! Yes, you!" it was a captain and he was shouting at me. I stopped and turned around to look at him. "Where are you going with those prisoners?"

Where indeed?

I had to think of something fast as the guard captain now walked towards me with some suspicion. So far I had passed as a Cathor guard transporting prisoners to the street level, but obviously by the sound of the captain's voice I had to have a valid reason to be taking any prisoner—much less three of them—*out* of the prison. The captain was now standing in front of me and eyeing me with some suspicion.

"Where are you going with those prisoners?" he growled at me. "I see they are from Aboola, the three spies. They are not permitted to leave the prison!"

"Yes, Captain, you are correct," I told him carefully effecting a boasting manner, then pointing to their bruises, "but they have told me what I need to know. They gave me secret information that I must immediately tell only to the emperor or his ministers."

The captain looked at me curiously, then at their bruised faces, bruises they had received when they had been captured and imprisoned, and he smiled broadly, "So you made them talk, then?"

I smiled, nodded knowingly.

The captain was impressed by my supposed brutality to my prisoners.

"Warrior," he told me on the side, "I can not come with you now as my men have a duty we must perform, but take care, these Aboolas are slippery fiends. Good work, and do not forget to mention my name to the emperor or his ministers. I am called Pondog."

"I surely will do so, captain," I told him with a lusty grin. Then I pushed Beeg, Onat and Saad forward, "Come on you lazy *zibas*, move quickly now!"

"Remember, my name is Pondog. Captain Pondog."

"Oh, I shall not forget you, captain," I replied truthfully hiding a sly grin, then I began to move my phony prisoners out of the building. When we were near the doorway the captain suddenly called for me to stop and soon he was coming over to me.

What now, I thought?

"I have changed my mind and decided to accompany you to the palace," he told me arrogantly, for while not being too bright he must have finally seen a way he could take the credit for the prisoner's information. I could see the look on Beeg's face, but I could say nothing, otherwise the captain would become suspicious. So now the captain also accompanied us.

Pondog told me proudly, "I will leave my men, they can have their fun and torture the new prisoners, but I will come with you to the palace. Just myself, as I have a stake in this."

CHAPTER 11

What stake did he have in this, I wondered? Then I realized the truth and just nodded. There was nothing I could do about it now.

"I am Pondog, captain of the City East Gate, not an officer of the prison," he told me with gruff pride, by way of explanation. So he was not of the prison. That was interesting. I just nodded, mumbled, "Glad you are with us, captain."

He looked at me more closely, "I have never seen you before, warrior. What is your name?"

"Tan," I replied firmly, hoping he was not familiar with all the warriors in the huge prison. Apparently he was not. I breathed a sigh or relief.

He said nothing more on the subject but only spoke about himself, obviously his favorite subject. We marched our charges through the city to the Florian Palace. To hear Pondog you would think he was the greatest warrior in all of Cathor. I found the company of the man unbearable. He was a braggart and probably a bully, but not a true fighter at all. He had no honor at all either. He actually took pride in relating stories where he had killed and tortured innocent women and children. He gloated in the gory details. He was a bore and a coward and he was getting on my nerves. That any city would allow such a fiend to be an officer in their city guard told me all I needed to know about how low Cathor had sunk under it's present leadership. I began to have my doubts about my mission here. Nevertheless, I had to play my part, so laughing at his horrid jokes, and agreeing with his outrageous shameful statements, I did so as not to make him suspicious. I even kicked my three 'prisoners' once, for Cathors are not known at all for their humane treatment of prisoners. Pondog approved of my action, in fact, he thought it too lenient. I also shouted at my charges to keep their mouths shut—for I could easily see how they felt about Pondog's words. And they were fighting hard to keep their emotions in check and play their part in my little ruse.

We walked down many streets and wide boulevards, eventually crossing the entire length of the city, but Captain Pondog did not seem the least suspicious now, he just kept on gloating over the honors he would receive for bringing *his* prisoners to the palace to give *his* secret information to the emperor. He did not even care what that information might be. He never even asked me. I was astounded by his lack of interest, but much relieved for it. It saved me from having to think up some false but reasonable form of secret information. Whatever that might be!

"Perhaps, if we are lucky, we shall even be permitted to watch the torture of these three spies?" Pondog stated, with a wide anticipatory grin.

I looked at him and only could nod, staying in character, "Perhaps?"

"Do not worry, Tan," Pondog told me gloating with anticipation of some promotion, no doubt, "the strongest man always wins, but I shall mention to the emperor you had your own small part in all this."

"Thank you," I told him trying to keep my sarcasm down.

"Of course, that is only fair, and I am a fair fellow. Ask anyone," he smiled, much impressed with himself.

"So that is why you chose to accompany me, alone. Not bringing your men?"

"Of course, I saw an opportunity, and took it." he told me proudly. "They would only get in the way."

"Perhaps you are right," I answered.

"You know that I am."

"Well, I am just doing my job," I smiled and told him calmly, suppressing my rage at the very audacity of the fellow.

"Good to hear that, Tan. That is the way to be," he told me, now more sure of himself, smiling broadly with victory, that I would not make any trouble for him. "Too bad I do not have more warriors like you under my command. All I have are lazy complainers."

I smiled grimly, "They just take advantage of your good nature."

"Exactly!" Pondog exclaimed loudly as if he had suddenly discovered some amazing fact, not getting my sarcasm at all, or not caring.

Beeg, Onat and Saad looked at him in utter astonishment and then looked at me with grim smiles. I looked back at them and allowed a sly grin, then told them, "Come on you lazy scum! Move!"

Soon the Florian Palace, home of the Cathor emperors for uncounted centuries, came into view as we turned a corner on the prestigious Imperial Boulevard. The Palace was impressive, gargantuan, and even beautiful, an ornate edifice of such exquisite grandeur there was none to rival it anywhere on our world. It fairly took your breathe away. It was a magnificent tribute to ostentatious excess and imperial success.

The three Aboolas and myself were visibly impressed with the palace, but Pondog hardly even noticed the lithe turrets, regal towers, and glorious spires of gold, crusted with precious stones. These caused the building to glitter in the sun light like a glowing beacon. It was an incredible structure that accommodated the emperor, his family, his retinue, the royal court, and all manner of city government officials. It was also heavily guarded, for upon Rigel assassination is always a threat for any leader. The grand building stood alone in a large area of well-cultivated grounds with a tall wall that surrounded it. It looked inaccessible.

There were trees and nearby out-buildings on the property that were close to the wall. I noticed that, for later. They might make things less difficult if the situation broke badly for us. I was not feeling too optimistic the closer we came to the palace. The only way into the building seemed to be through the main gate. As it turned out, this is where Captain Pondog made himself useful.

I had an uneasy feeling about walking up to the gate of the palace to seek entrance, but with Captain Pondog leading us, there was no trouble at all. It seems he was known, and feared, and always obeyed. As it worked out Pondog knew the guards there well and we were allowed to pass inside immediately. In fact, we had two of the guards from the gate accompany us into the very presence of the emperor. My concern was for naught, for all the palace guards did was speak quickly with Pondog, ignoring me and the prisoners. I began to wonder how such a cowardly fool and blowhard could have any friends at all!

I shall not bore you with all the details, but suffice it to say that we were led through the various beautifully decorated halls and corridors until we came to the grand throne room of Cathor. It was an enormous chamber of gigantic proportions and probably was used to accommodate throngs of people. Now it was only occupied by a few men.

As we entered the huge room I saw a throne at the far end and upon it sat Kantor, Emperor of Cathor. I was not impressed. He was an old husk of a man and obviously in ill health. He had wished for a son to be his heir but instead had none, and this with his age and ill health had broken his spirit. He was nowhere near the strong ruler it was said he had once been a long time ago. He had become a drab withered old man holding no outstanding characteristics of leadership, other than that he held the office of emperor in his shaky grasping hands. It was a sad sight to behold such a once gifted leader reduced to senile incompetence.

Surrounding the emperor, on both sides of the elegant throne, stood half a dozen of his most powerful ministers, most of them drab little men like himself, relics of an earlier age. Many years before, they might have been steady fighting men, but today they were a sad sight to look upon. Here our two guards left us, saying farewell to Pondog and we were told to approach the throne by a palace lackey.

As my eyes were directed to the emperor, my glance could not keep away from noticing one of the men at his side. He was a much younger man, tall and thin, with black hair and a long thin black beard. It gave him a most cruel appearance. He was also looking at me, and I saw a grim smile come to his face. I wondered what that might mean and was sure it was not a good sign. Beeg could not restrain a mocking tone as we moved closer to the emperor.

"What is it you want of our emperor?" the black haired man asked in a powerful voice that was used to wielding power.

Before Pondog could get a word out, I gave the signal and Beeg, Saad and Onat loosened their bonds. Beeg quickly knocked Pondog aside as he took his sword.

Now the four of us were armed and ready for any eventuality.

The palace guard was slow to act, so we acted immediately.

"Great Kartor," I spoke up forcefully. "We have very important news to give you. It concerns your city and your life."

"What is the meaning of this?" the emperor snapped, but more curious than angry. It was obvious he did not entirely realize what was going on. His mind had not alerted him to the fact that this might be some assassination attempt. I quickly got his attention.

"The Zorrs have a plan to conqueror your city and take away your throne," I told him loudly so all there could clearly hear my words. "Hold back your men, great emperor! Listen to what I have to say. It is in your interest, and Cathor's, that you do so."

My words seemed to interest the emperor as it would any man of power who constantly feared for his life and position. He knew he could always have us cut down later if he so desired. He did not seem to fear us and we did not move to threaten him. With a withered hand he signaled his guards to hold off against us. They stopped instantly, but stood by, ever ready with swords out should there be any assassination attempt. Fully a hundred of the guards were soon standing by surrounding us and ready to be called in against us, but as yet they were holding back but with drawn swords. There were also at least 20 archers ready to cut us down if given the word. These were the real danger to us.

"Then speak quickly man, and if it be a lie or some plot, you shall regret it," Kartor said looking deeply at the four of us intently.

"I have a long story to tell you, but I shall keep it short, great emperor," I said forcefully. "My friends and I have traveled a far distance to bring you this news. It is very important to your safety and the safety of your city. Will you allow us to speak our words in safety? Will you hold your decision at least until we have finished our words?"

"No!" the dark man at his side shouted. "It is some kind of devilish plot. Kill them now, My Emperor! End their danger to your life. They have the audacity to break into your presence, and then dare dictate terms to you! What they want to do is kill you!"

"That is a dirty lie!" I growled looking squarely into the eyes of the bearded man.

'A lie? I think not," he said forcefully.

"Emperor, we only seek to tell you the truth, a truth you must hear," I said, with more meaning than I had ever expressed before. It must have worked.

"I think I will hear these men out, loyal Koth," the emperor said in a tired tone. He was alert and interested, for now, but how long he would be so I could not know. I had to talk fast.

Then my companions and I told our story to the emperor and all those in that massive hall of the palace in Cathor. I spoke about the Zel Clan, the Zorr Gold Ring wearers and their secret outlaw society, their stronghold in the Hills of Mystery, and their enemy the Togs. I told of the Zorr plan for conquest of Cathor, and of their strength and power that was growing and would soon control all the free cities of Rigel.

Koth spoke up in dismissal, saying he knew the Zorr cult well, and what we said was no news, and they were no serious danger. He also added that he knew the Zel Clan was behind all this trouble. Then he looked at me and said, "Are you one of these traitorous Zels?"

"No! You know that I am not. If you think so, you are a fool or a liar!" I told him boldly.

"Enough of this bickering!" Kartor told us, annoyed and growing more restive. "Continue your words quickly, young man, and then I shall rule. However, be forewarned, it may not be the decision you seek. We are very hard on traitors and assassins and their plots here in Cathor."

I gulped nervously, nodded, concentrating on the matter at hand. "So be it, sire, you must gather your military forces and attack the stronghold of the Zorrs and end their power forever. They must be destroyed, and their leader, who is only known as Zorr, must be captured and exposed for what he is. They are a danger to your rule. You must also allow the Zels back into favor in Cathor and restore their lands and authority. They are not traitors; they include some of your most loyal allies who oppose the Zorrs."

"No!" Kartor said finally on that point, "the Zels are traitors, isn't that right, Koth?"

Koth merely nodded with a grim smile. "Of course. The emperor is most wise."

"I THINK I WILL HEAR THESE MEN OUT..."

Then Koth moved close to the old man and whispered in his ear. Both men now nodded knowingly.

I looked at my three companions, knowing I might have ruined our chances by bringing up the subject of the Zels. Feelings on them were still harsh in Cathor.

Koth now smiled at me and spoke up. "Intruder, what you say about this enemy stronghold may be true. Some of my spies recently have told me of a traitorous group of outlaws hiding in the hills that should be wiped out."

'They are strong and there are many thousands of them," I added, wondering what this Koth might be up to, but at least I was relieved that he now seemed to be championing our cause to attack the outlaws in the Hills of Mystery.

"No matter," Koth said with a grim look at me that sent an ominous chill through my bones. I do not know why I had that feeling about him. I certainly had no dire reason for it. "These outlaws shall all be destroyed."

I nodded. That was good to hear.

Then he asked, "What is your name, warrior?"

"Prince Tan Alvaka of Asudra," I replied to Koth and all in that great chamber who now looked at me more carefully.

"A prince of Asudra? I knew you were not a Cathor," he proclaimed loudly with some malice. "No doubt a Zel, or one of their partners. An outlaw and an enemy. Well, we shall see. Perhaps you would like to ride with our army to this stronghold and see how we deal with this enemy?"

I said that I would be most willing to be part of such a military force. Even honored. Then I asked if Beeg, Onat and Saad would be allowed their freedom to return to Aboola.

"Granted," Kartor said, perhaps too magnanimously. "All is granted. The three men from Aboola may leave us now. First Minister Koth, tomorrow, you will make plans to send our army to attack these outlaws and defeat them once and for all."

"The outlaws shall be destroyed, My Emperor," Koth told his sovereign most obediently, and perhaps with too much flourish. Nevertheless, things seemed to be working out as I wanted them to, so I could not complain. Nevertheless, I had a nagging feeling that all was not well. It seemed to me some kind of sneaky trick might be in the works, but I dared not speak my true feelings at that time. This man, Koth, seemed to be a slimy one for certain, but most of these high officials were like that. He was First Minister of Cathor, perhaps the real power behind the throne? I wondered what his game might be.

"Do not underestimate these outlaws," I added to Koth by way of warning. "They are well armed and organized. They control the lands adjoining the Hills of Mystery and their stronghold seems impregnable, with secret exits and entrances."

Koth just nodded, smiling as if he knew something that I did not.

The audience was over and the major domo of the palace bade us leave.

On the way out I said my farewells to Beeg, Onat and Saad. We shook hands and I gave them a wily grin, "It was a pleasure to be a prisoner with each one of you."

"Yes, a real pleasure, Tan. We will have to do it again, sometime," Beeg spoke up with a grin.

We all just laughed and then they made ready to leave.

"If you ever come to Aboola," Beeg told me, "Just ask for Beeg Alon and anyone will tell you where to find me. My house, is your house, my friend."

Onat and Saad told me the same. I thanked them and then they left.

And with that the three men from Aboola were gone from the Florian Palace and my sight. They had proved good fellows and I wished them well. I hoped to meet them again. Some day.

Meanwhile, after my audience with the emperor I was given a large chamber in the palace to rest for the evening, before we got started to make plans to attack the stronghold the next morning. There was good food brought forth, and I needed and appreciated it all before we left to deal with the Zorrs. For tomorrow we would make ready the attack on the stronghold of the enemy and take down their power forever.

That night before I slept, I was determined to see Lady Dallia once more. Evidently she was of some sort of noble birth, and I had no way to find her whereabouts in the city. I asked about her in the palace, but men and women there, of high birth and low, did not seem to know who she might be. Or they would not tell me. I found that most strange. In fact, it did not make any sense that such a beautiful and noble lady would not be known. It seemed as if some word had gone out and that no one wanted me to find her. I wondered why. I had limited time before we left the city to fight the Zorr horde. I could not knock on the door of every nobleman's house in Cathor and it was late now. I decided to search her out tomorrow, early in the morning, before the plans for the attack were made and finalized.

CHAPTER 12

The next morning, I awoke with a loud knock on the door of my room. It was a Cathor captain of the guards, and as I cleared the sleep from my eyes, I saw him more clearly and suddenly realized it was that braggart, sadistic Captain Pondog himself. He sneered at me with an evil grin.

"First Minister Koth," Pondog told me with a sly look, "requests your presence at his palace. There the ministers and commanders of Cathor will meet to map out their strategy to attack the enemy stronghold. Hurry now, for I have many good ideas to tell these ministers."

"I am sure that you do," I said as I quickly got dressed.

Pondog proved to be the same arrogant fool as ever, as I slipped on my clothes and fighting harness. Once we left the Florian Palace on our walk to Koth's palace, Pondog asked me, seemingly most curiously, why I had lied to him.

I countered by asking him, why is it that he seemed not to be mad that I lied to him. "After all," I added carefully, "I tricked you and escaped from the prison."

Pondog just grinned, then spoke up frankly. "At first I was mad and would have killed you. I had heard stories of how the emperor spoke that one day he would raid the outlaw stronghold. I saw an excellent opportunity to put myself in the good graces of the emperor and his ministers. Perhaps I shall even be put in command of the attacking army?"

"Perhaps you shall," I replied, hiding my sarcasm at his unimaginable arrogance.

It seemed that Pondog set his sights extremely high and judging by his personality I knew he would never get that command. I did wonder though, who would get it? Definitely not Pondog, I was sure. He was a coward and lackey, and incompetent at best. I wondered who would be put in command of the attacking army, and if he would be up to the task of destroying the cult of Zorr?

Soon we came to another palace that belonged to First Minister Koth. It was truly magnificent and rivaled the beauty and grace of the Florian Palace itself.

As Pondog led me into Koth's palace, we met more guards, and we were escorted into a large atrium and then down a long corridor that led into a large meeting hall.

Here we found First Minister Koth and many of the emperor's other ministers and officers I had seen the day before. They were engaged in a heated discussion. There were also a dozen generals and officers of the Cathor army, all seated around an enormous table. Pondog and I were acknowledged rather snidely by Koth when we entered, and then were pointed to seats off to the side, away from the table. And out of the way.

It took many *tals* for them to get their plan organized and set, Koth finally asked me to speak of what I knew. I told them of the exact location of the enemy stronghold, it's defenses, numbers of entrances and the amount of fighting men I had seen there.

"They are good warriors and will give your men strong opposition," I told them, offering all the information I knew to ensure our success. "You will need to send a large force of no less than five thousand warriors to do the job properly."

After I gave my report, they generally haggled over various parts of their plan for a long while. The fact that the Cathors underestimated this enemy was obvious to me now, but not to any of them. That worried me. They did not seem to have sound judgment, or listen to good advice, or perhaps they did not care. Finally, I succeeded in convincing them that a force of nothing less than five thousand trained warriors would be necessary to ensure victory.

At first, they refused to approve a force of that many men, but then Koth came to my aid.

"Prince Tan speaks wisely. I think a force of that amount would be exactly what is needed," Koth spoke up firmly. He looked at me and nodded. I could not believe it, but I was glad for his support. Perhaps he was coming around? Nevertheless, I could not help feeling uneasy in his presence. There was something unsettling about the man.

"Warriors! I know there is no real threat to Cathor," Koth suddenly spoke up in a calm relaxed voice, "but perhaps a force of five thousand would do the trick, as this Tan Alvaka says. Or at least it would be large enough to crush any conceivable opposition a few paltry outlaws might give us. We would have enough men to surround and block off these outlaws, making it possible to catch or kill them all."

I agreed, generally, but wondered about his support.

Soon a plan was agreed on. Five thousand warriors under General Len Le would leave tomorrow in secret for the Hills of Mystery. The stronghold would be surrounded, and all known exits would be blocked. I knew where two were located and told them. However, that would not be so easy to trap all these creatures for we only knew of two portals, and there certainly were others.

Once the portals were blocked, none of the enemy could escape, then we could enter the stronghold and destroy the Zorr threat forever. Or so we hoped. It seemed to be a sound plan. One that must work. Soon they were bickering on all minor questions. I shrugged and left them to their own devices, left the meeting room of Koth's house, walking down a long elaborate corridor to go back to my own quarters in the Florian Palace. It was then that I was stunned as my eyes fell upon a beautiful blonde haired young lady walking through the front gardens. It was the Lady Dallia! I had finally found her, and I was overjoyed as I ran to meet her.

I'm afraid I was too excited, for her back was towards me and as I came near her, she jumped with a start. She turned around startled and when she saw me, her face turned to a large, beautiful smile. We both stood there, most surprised to see each other, neither knowing what to say to the other for the moment but smiling with great joy that we had found each other. It is a feeling you cannot know unless love strikes you head-on.

"Oh, Tan!" she cried out, running towards me with her arms opened to embrace me. "I thought I would never see you again when the guards took you away. I tried to help you get out of that prison, but I could do nothing. My father would hear none of it."

I did not care about any of that now. For that short moment I held her in my arms, and we kissed hungrily. It was wonderful. Afterwards she looked at me with serious concern.

"But what are you doing here?" she asked with curious surprise. "My love, this is a dangerous place for you."

"Well might I ask you that very same questions." I said as I looked upon her, she looked radiant in that environment. "What are you doing in this house?"

"Why, I live here," she said simply.

I looked at her now deeply curious, "Koth? He is your father?"

She nodded and smiled.

I tried to hold back my dismay. Even though Koth seemed loyal, he was not likeable. I did not trust him, even if I had no proof of any treachery from him. He seemed loathsome to me and treacherous, nor had I forgotten that he was the man who had ordered a warrior to bodily fetch Lady Dallia back from the market to his home, like a common slave girl. I was astonished that such a fair and beautiful woman like Dallia could have such a loathsome creature as Koth for her father."

"Well, Koth is not really my father," Dallia explained to my query with a sad look upon her face. "Actually, he is my stepfather, and he is a beast, and a very bad man."

"I see that in him as well," I replied as we stood there alone. "I do not trust him at all, but he seems to be loyal to the emperor. I can not find any evidence of his treachery, and he is supporting the army in the attack against the Zorrs."

"That may be true, or not. He is very smart and cunning," Dallia told me in warning.

Then I told her about the attack on the Zorr stronghold and that I would have to leave her soon to join the fight. She was very sad at hearing this news. It was good to know that she worried about me and cared about me. Just knowing that lifted my spirits.

"I think I love you, Tan," she whispered in a sultry voice, as we held each other so closely. "Ever since I saw you in the marketplace, you were so brave, and you saved my life twice that day."

"I feel the same way about you, Dallia," I told her in a soft voice, then looked at her sadly. "But I am afraid I will not be able to be with you until this Zorr crisis is over. Their power must be destroyed. Many of my friends have died already fighting their evil."

Just then a harsh voice from behind us called Dallia's name. We turned and saw Koth coming towards us red with anger.

"Get over here!" he demanded a bit too forcefully. "Both of you!"

I did not like his words or manner and told him so.

As we walked over, once Koth realized that it was I who was with Dallia, he seemed to calm down somewhat. He even smiled, but his smile had a wicked leer to it.

"First you disobey me and go to the market against my orders," he said sternly to Dallia. "Once there, you get involved in a riot with this Asudra criminal. Now I see you embracing in his arms! Remember, you are promised to another! Now go to your room immediately!"

I could see that Dallia was visibly hurt by his words, yet she looked like she expected it and she bore it well. As she walked away to her room, she looked back at Koth.

"You were my father's best friend and I thought because of that you would be good to me. I was wrong, you are a vile beast! Always you seek to keep me locked away on these palace grounds. You cannot tell me what to do forever!"

Then Dallia stormed out of the corridor and went to her rooms.

After she left Koth turned towards me. I was disgusted at the way he had treated Dallia but said nothing. Yet I promised myself there would be a day of reckoning soon when my sword would do my talking for me.

"And you, prince of Asudra," he said to me in heated anger. "Do not try my patience. I know it was you who fought for Dallia in the marketplace and that you slew a dozen of my armed men. Do not allow your mission against Zorr to become sidetracked by any interest in Dallia. As I have already said, she is promised to another. You are to stay away from her. This is a warning. And I warn you, my patience is limited. The next time you shall not fare so well. Now be gone from my sight!"

Then before I could reply he strode back further into his palace and left me there in the atrium alone to think upon his words.

I was fuming with anger. How anyone, least of all a father, even if only a stepfather, could treat Dallia in such a manner was beyond me to comprehend. I was enraged at his treatment of her, but I kept myself under control. For now. I left Koth's palace and headed back to my rooms at the emperor's palace.

As I strode back to the Florian Palace, back to my room within the massive structure, I could not get Dallia off my mind. I had to see her again, no matter what the consequences. I did not care what Koth said and began to think of a plan whereby to secretly enter Koth's palace and make my way to her chambers. I knew it might mean death for me if I was caught, for Koth had been clear on the consequences of such a reckless action, but I did not dwell upon any such consequences where Dallia was concerned. I had faced death many times, in many horrible guises, but I should accept those consequences contentedly if it was for even a smile from my Lady Dallia's lovely lips.

I waited for some time when it was dark, then I briskly walked back to Koth's palace. All was quiet in the area now, for the attack had been scheduled for the next day and all forces would be ready to move the next morning. So, I still had plenty of time. I was strong in my conviction to see Dallia once more before I left to go into battle. I had to see her. I knew Koth was lawfully within his rights to stop me from seeing her, for as her legal guardian he had complete lawful power over her. He could easily have me killed, and not one word of disapproval would be uttered by the powers that be. Many parents on Rigel arrange marriages for their children, usually to enlarge their own family power. In my home city of Asudra, it is realized that this is wrong, and all young people have the right to choose their own mate. In other cities, the young were not so free, such as Cathor.

As I neared Koth's palace I noticed a large and wiry *ubor* tree close to the window of Dallia's rooms, which she had earlier pointed out to me. I noticed guards at the gate, so quietly I crept around to the gardens and silently climbed over the wall. Then concealing myself from detection, I swiftly made my way to the large *ubor* tree. It was tall and wiry and would be hard for me to climb, for my people are not a climbing people, but I would find a way and climb it nonetheless.

The tree was easily some fifty or more *haads* straight upwards, and so little by little I climbed higher and higher to my goal. Soon Dallia came to the window, surprised at first but very happy to see me. Her smile made my heart sing with joy.

"Make haste, Tan," she told me quickly, "the guards patrol will come by this way soon and they will see you."

Finally, I reached the window sill. Then I pulled myself upwards and Dallia helped me as I pulled myself through her window and into her room. I saw the guards patrolling the palace grounds passing below. They had not seen me.

"That was close," I said as I entered Dallia's room and held her close to me.

"Welcome to my prison, my love," she told me with a sad smile. "Why did you come? Do you not know that Koth will have you killed for this?"

"I had to see you before I leave for battle tomorrow," I replied softly as I held her in my arms, and neither of us let go for a long moment.

Later, as we talked together, I noticed Dallia's room. It was exceedingly plain even desolate, very much like a prison cell, consisting only of a bed, table, chair, and a large closet for clothing. It was sparse and grim. It seemed Koth kept her as a virtual prisoner though I could not understand why. Dallia told me that for some unknown reason Koth seemed to despise her, and it seemed the only reason Koth took her in as a little girl child was to satisfy his own hatred and pleasure at beating her when she was disobedient. My anger grew red hot at hearing these words, but I kept my voice silent for fear of disturbing her more.

I asked Dallia about her real father, but she did not remember him. When her mother died Koth had taken her in. Her mother's name was Albea.

"I have heard it said that Koth wanted my mother to be his wife, but she hated him and when she would not come to him in marriage, under some government order, he had my father and brothers sent away and took Albea in secrecy. She became his captive." she said sadly.

I further learned that although very young at the time, Dallia saw her mother kill herself rather than submit to the affections of Koth. Afterwards she was raised by a female servant in a secluded arm of the palace. It was only recently that she had even seen Koth again, for she had not seen him since childhood.

A mighty hatred grew within me at the monster that was Koth. How anyone could be so cruel and vile I could hardly understand. I shook my head in determination that Koth's hold over her would be forever broken.

Then I asked her, "What of this story that you are promised to another?"

"Yes, it is true. I am promised to Selek, the emperor of the city of Bamhor," she told me with a terse voice. "He is a horrid man, but he is a friend of Koth. I shall never go to his city—nor his bed! I will destroy myself rather than submit!"

"Do not worry, "I told her firmly. "I will not let them take you."

"But I am supposed to be sent to Bamhor in just two *talas!*" she said with much despair. A period of two days and nights time.

"Then we will have to go away from here before that time arrives," I told her in a firm voice. "We can go to my city of Asudra, and I will take you there soon. But first I must take my place in the attack against Zorr that is set for the next morning."

I had told Dallia what I had found out about the Zorrs and their leader, as well as about my friends Droth and Hotath, whom now I presumed to be dead, and she understood completely the seriousness of my mission.

"I will wait for you, Tan Alvaka of Asudra," she told me with a sad look in her eyes, a look of caring and deep love. It graced my heart. I smiled, then she added, "I know you will come for me, but you must come before those two *talas* pass, for I shall not let them send me to Bamhor."

I understood the meaning of her words all too well. I would make sure that the fate of the daughter, would not repeat that of the mother.

Just then the doors to Dallia's rooms, which had been locked from the outside—like a prison cell—opened to admit a score of Koth's guards. They saw me there and came at me with drawn swords.

"Surrender!" their leader shouted at me. "Surrender and by Lord Koth's word you shall not be killed."

I looked to Dallia and I could see her fear that I would fight and die right there in front of her, for there were too many of them for me to fight off effectively. I nodded reluctantly. There seemed nothing I could do for there were too many of them, but the most important reason I did not fight was that in all the confusion of clashing blades, I feared for my Lady Dallia's safety. Carefully I threw my weapons to the floor, and then my hands were tied as I was led outside of Dallia's rooms into a long corridor. Dallia, clinging to me, sobbing with sadness and anger, was thrown to the floor of her chamber roughly by the guard leader.

"You will pay for that!" I growled at him, as I tried to reach him with a hard fist. But it was not to be.

I was dragged out of the room and then the door to Dallia's rooms was locked behind me.

"You will regret that!" I told the guard once again. "Mark my words!"

He just laughed and kicked me a few times to move me along the hallway more quickly.

CHAPTER 13

I was unarmed, bound and led to what fate I did not know. I questioned my guards but all I got in response were grim laughs and a few more punches. They were a nasty bunch. I was being led down a long corridor which I finally could see took us into the stables of Koth's palace.

There I met Pondog, who with his usual twisted attitude proceeded to slap me some more while he laughed heartily. He seemed to find it all very funny. I held myself in check, for the moment. I was bound and unable to fight back. His time would come.

"Pondog, have these men release me at once!" I demanded. "I am to be in the attack on the enemy stronghold and they are to leave soon."

He just laughed some more as if he knew something that I did not. I was sure he was correct. Pondog had proved to be a very sly fellow.

I knew that it would soon be the time when the army would leave Cathor and ride to attack the enemy stronghold. I noticed that many of the warriors were beginning to leave already, others forming up into companies.

"You are a fool, Tan Alvaka," Pondog finally told me as mounts were being brought over to us. "You played right into our hands—a true fool—even a much bigger fool that ever we thought you would be."

"What is all this? What are you talking about?" I shouted full of rage. I was angry and still bound and did not understand what was happening. Nor why. This seemed much more serious than me sneaking into Dallia's room for a private moment in Koth's palace. This was something else altogether!

"Where are you taking me, you arrogant *foog*?" I demanded, using the word *foog* was a most grievous insult, being derived from a root word having to do with vile excrement that had a particularly disgusting odor. It fit Pondog very well.

For this word of insult, I was repeatedly punched until my body was aching all over. Then the mounts were brought to us. Enormous *zibas* that were specially bred for war.

"You, my dear friend, Prince Tan Alvaka," he snarled at me with a twisted grin, "are to be taken before Zorr himself, and may the almighty god Ibar have mercy on you when The Master gets through with you."

"Who is this man who calls himself Zorr?" I asked, my curiousity as always, getting the better of me. I looked forward to my meeting with him, and perhaps, I would take him captive if possible—but that was a moot point now as I was the one who was the captive.

Pondog and his men only laughed. They saw my words quite amusing. It was not long before we were on our mounts and were on our way out of the city. Surprisingly our party had no trouble leaving Cathor, and no guards questioned us as we made our way through the city even though it was obvious I was a captive. What Cathor warrior would logically question another, especially a captain in the military harness of First Minister Koth? Or so it seemed. As we rode north, I saw a large tree, underneath of which was a small building. It appeared to be a farmhouse but as we entered, an old man came out to the leaders of my captors and gave them all black robes and hoods with silver face masks with horrid designs to wear. They all dressed in this new clothing and wore masks. They looked fearsome and terrible. Then I saw Pondog slip a Bronze Ring upon his finger. Now I knew for sure! The hated ring of Zorr! My heart sank so deeply, I had been so easily tricked and betrayed. Now what of Cathor and their army?

Zorr spies must surely know of the attack coming on their stronghold, which was where we were supposed to be headed. What I could not fathom was why did this Zorr want *me*? What was my importance? Once our army reached the stronghold, it would be a close battle. Even if Zorr knew of the attack upon his organization in the Hills of Mystery, and that I had promoted this battle to the emperor, with Len Le's five thousand man force—the Cathor army should be able to easily overcome the mere thousand warriors of Zorr. My thoughts were fearful though. I wondered if they would be taken by surprise? Would the enemy be ready and waiting for us? Was there more to this than I knew? Or more of the enemy than we knew? Obviously, anything was possible. I began to fear we had been betrayed by vile treachery since the beginning of this entire enterprise. These were the thoughts that were going on within my mind. And as always, the safety of my Lady Dallia was centermost in my thoughts. Where was she and what was happening to her now?

Perhaps some of this sinister action was being done to get back at me? I wondered about that. It did not seem likely, as I was not important at all in the grand scheme of things. I hoped it might only be some minor kind of personal dislike. That was possible too. Regardless, after my captors were dressed in their dark Zorr robes and gruesome face masks, we left the way station and our mounts raced swiftly northward once more.

Our party made good time. We rode hard all night, and by early morning we had made it to the border of the Hills of Mystery. It seemed we arrived only scant hours before the Cathor army were due to get there to begin their attack upon the stronghold. I did not understand, it almost seemed the Zorrs *wanted* the Cathors to attack their stronghold! Then I realized that might have been their plan all along. I had been used as a pawn and the information I provided the old emperor had been twisted for use against him and his army. It had caused a military action that would lead to a trap and utter defeat for Cathor. Then, with the troops loyal to the city killed or captured, Cathor could be open to be conquerored by the forces of Zorr. It is as if they come from the very Underworld itself! I raged at the realization. I had to do something to stop it! But what? I was still bound and helpless, and under guard.

There seemed to be guards posted everywhere looking down onto the plains watching all the paths and roads. Evidently the enemy knew full well of the pending attack and were watching our movements. They were ready to spring their trap.

We entered the stronghold, riding in slowly and carefully. The large portal had been left open, a certain worry of a trap that I told the commander. No one listened to me. I looked inside the stronghold, everything appeared quiet, and I was astonished to see so few guards throughout the place. These were quickly taken care of as we rode inside. It appeared the place was deserted. With myself under guard and still with my hands tied, I was once again brought into the Great Hall where I had first seen Zorr long ago. The huge hall was completely empty now. No one was in sight as I was led to what appeared to be a simple blank wall. Here Pondog evidently began searching for something on the wall and soon a large portion of the apparent solid rock slid back revealing a opening with steps that led upward into a corridor beyond. Here we dismounted our *zibas* and as a couple of warriors took charge of our mounts, the remaining of my group of captors and myself walked up the steps of this secret passageway.

The steps were set in a large spiral which ran up the inside of the wall of the Great Hall. We walked up dozens of steps until finally we saw a light beyond at the top and a closed door with a guard. Pondog spoke some words, obviously some sort of password, and soon we were admitted.

I was led into a large room, that was above the Great Hall, with a view that looked straight down into it. Then I finally saw Zorr himself, safely concealed in his robes and mask to hide his true identity. I could tell it was him though. I wondered who he might be.

Soon I was brought to a wall and chained to it by my hands and feet.

"Great Zorr!" Pondog announced to me with bluster. "He wishes to allow you to see the destruction of the Cathor army, *before* you are executed."

"That is nice of him," I mocked tersely.

Pondog just laughed in joyous cruelty.

There were dozens of warriors in that room, mostly Gold Ring, Silver Ring and Bronze Ring wearers, all conferring with their leader. I was chained there for some time until Zorr finished with his meeting and came over to me.

"Ah, yes, it is the constant annoyance known as Prince Tan Alvaka," the voice mocked grimly as he looked down upon me, but there was something about that voice that seemed familiar to me. Yet I could not place it. Perhaps it was because the hood and golden face mask obscured his voice? Then he continue in a sharp tone. "You once again have come to visit us—though not in the manner you anticipated. I do hope that you will make your stay longer this time—until it is time when I decide to end your life."

"You dirty piece of rotting foog!" I shouted enraged. "You will pay for all your crimes!"

He did not appreciate that defiance and came over to me and slapped my face. Then he ordered all his men to leave the room for a moment. I was unsure what he meant to do, and then it came to me. Once we were alone, he surprised me by pulling back his black hood, and taking off his face mask, to reveal to me his true identity. I was shocked, astounded. Then it all made sense to me. He laughed in my face with an ominous tone that seemed to ooze pure evil.

I growled back in righteous anger, my face contorted into a grim masque of shock and outrage. Yes, I recognized that face! It was a face that I loathed, for it belonged to a man that I hated above all others now. It was the face of First Minister Koth of Cathor! It was Lady Dallia's own stepfather! I was shocked and could not believe the baseless treachery of the man, and now I could plainly tell that his voice matched the voice that I had heard earlier belonging to the mysterious man known only as Zorr.

"It will not harm me now to show you my true self," he told me with vicious pride and arrogant hatred, "for you shall not live long enough to make use of such knowledge."

"So you are Zorr!" I shouted, rattling my chains against the wall, wishing I could wrap them around his neck. "You are nothing but a dirty treacherous traitor! Why? Why are you doing all this?"

I could not believe it, but it was true. It was First Minister Koth of Cathor who was the leader of this secret society of outlaws and criminals. To his nefarious credit I could now well believe him capable of it all. He was a monster, just as the lovely Dallia had warned me. He was the leader of this deadly Zorr cult! Their plan was the conquest of every one of the free cities of Rigel. I cursed myself for a fool that I had not seen it all sooner. Now I was not only helpless and his prisoner again, but the invading army I had promoted to the emperor of Cathor was being led into a trap. As the light of realization dawned upon me that it had been Koth all along who had pressed for the invasion of the stronghold—it was a way to easily trap and destroy the army of Cathor! I knew now that our invading army had no chance. And I was here, helpless to warn them!

"SO YOU ARE ZORR!"

"Fool!" Koth shouted in almost a joyful tone. "You have done exactly what I hoped you would do. After you escaped my Pit of the Dead, I knew you would seek to enlist the aid of old Kartor, the emperor of Cathor, in your quest to destroy my organization. In this I played you well, even aided your quest with the emperor, and now in one crushing blow we destroy the pride of the army of Cathor and easily move to eventually conqueror the city. You have done much to aid my plans, Tan Alvaka. I should thank you."

I raged in anger at his arrogant but true words. He laughed again just to rub it in, then replaced his hood over his head and put on his face mask. Thus covered, he ordered his men back into the room. When his men had returned, he spoke with them for a moment. Then another warrior entered the room and spoke to him in a whisper. I saw him smile an evil grin.

"Very well! The time is at hand. Prepare yourselves, officers," he told the men there in that room. "The Cathor army is at the foot of the hills and ready to enter the stronghold and be destroyed. Lure them in here. Then kill them all!"

Quickly dozens of his officers left the room to attend to their units, as I looked down in the immense hall below. Koth was most generous for he had afforded a way whereby I could view the total destruction of the cream of the Cathor army.

Once again I cursed myself for a fool at having been tricked and then falling into Koth's clutches yet again. I vowed to escape and wreck all his plans—and I would end him once and for all, by stabbing my sword deeply into his guts!

At the time I could not help but think of my lovely Dallia and knew that I must get to her side and help her to escape this monster. But deep inside my heart I feared I would not be able to escape this place in order to help her. I feared I might never see her again. In one *tala* she would be sent to that fiend Selek of Bamhor—or destroy herself and be lost to me forever. What could I do to stop that?

My mind was in a whirl of clashing thoughts, a frenzy to escape from that place; save the Cathor army; and then save Dallia. It was too much to hope for, and I had no realistic expectation of success for any of it, but I would *make* it happen! I have always believed that all things are possible—or at least they can be *made* possible. I just had to find the way!

I thought about my options. Most probably by the time the battle was over I would also be dead. Murdered by Koth or his minions. Pondog would surely enjoy doing the deed, no doubt. Koth had no reason to keep me alive. I had lost my fight with the Zorrs and had let down my friends Droth and Hotath, but more than that I had let down my beloved Dallia. I fought feelings of overwhelming sadness and defeat—yet I would not accept any of it! There must be some way out of this!

"Prepare to watch the splendid slaughter," Pondog the arrogant told me, as he came close to me laughing with victory. "The Cathor army has already entered the stronghold and soon they shall be ours."

"General Len Le," I said with pride, "would not be so stupid as to extend his force so openly. Unprotected. No, they will not enter here and fall into your trap."

"You forget, Len Le is also one of our own men!" Pondog sneered gloatingly. This was something I had not known. Once again shock and anger clouded my mind at this news of even deeper treachery.

I feared all hope was lost then and I was now in a frenzy of despair. Len Le was one of Koth's men? It seemed incredible. He was a heroic and honored military man from an old and distinguished family. The very thought of his treachery revolted me. Where were the decent and honorable noblemen in Cathor? Were there any? Yes, there were, the five thousand brave warriors who were risking their lives here for Cathor. Yes, there were also the Zels, even though they themselves were outlawed. Old Kartor, who was too senile to realize the truth of the threat, had allowed Koth a free reign in his city's affairs. For a long time First Minister Koth, had almost complete control over the city. Soon he would own the city and it would all be his. Indeed, how could Koth lose, for had he not planned the attack, and was not Len Le his man?

CHAPTER 14

The Great Hall was empty now, yet I could hear the yells and curses of the Cathor warriors as they fought their way within the trap Koth had set for them. They thought they were trapping the Zorrs, but they were in fact fighting to get into a trap. It would be the doom of every one of them unless I could do something to change the outcome.

"You see," Pondog teased me with malicious glee, "Len Le has brought his entire army into our trap and soon that trap will be shut and the Cathor army shall be annihilated totally. Victory is sweet, is it not?"

I look at him and spit down at his feet.

"Now, now, that is not the proper way for a prince of the noble house of Alvaka to act," Pondog gloated over me.

I looked down once more into the Great Hall below and saw the first of the valiant Cathor warriors riding into the massive hall while more units of their troops came in through other entrances. The Great Hall was truly tremendous and could easily hold many thousands of fighters along with their huge mounts, with much room to spare.

Soon the hall was filled with over five thousand warriors of Cathor, most all mounted upon immense screeching *zibas* that were nervous and fearful at being ridden into an enclosed space. It seemed that the *zibas* could smell the trap, but their mounted warriors sadly could not. The trap had been set well, so even if the men told Len Le of their suspicions, it would be to no avail. All that was needed now was to spring the trap and seal their escape route.

When the last of the Cathors entered I saw Koth go to a panel and lower a number of levers. Instantly every exit in the Great Hall was sealed by large metal doors that came crashing down in a thunderous clang, trapping the entire Cathor army.

The success of the attack and my hopes for succor vanished when those doors came crashing down. Now all were trapped. They all knew it now and chaos reigned as I looked below, riders and beasts trampled and crashed against each other as they panicked and turned around to escape—but there was no place to escape to! Koth had planned well.

I wondered what Koth would do with his captives? It did not look like the brave Cathor warriors would be able to free themselves. I felt the dismal pall of doom overcoming them. It was terrible. What would Koth do? The Cathor army was trapped, true, but they were still alive and able to fight. Koth could not just leave them there. True they were trapped, but they were not helpless. There were five thousand highly trained armed warriors down there itching to fight. I had to find a way to help them get out of that trap. They were in the center of the Zorr stronghold and still posed a mighty threat to Koth and his outlaw cult.

I had to find some way to save them and bring victory out of defeat.

I noticed now that everyone in that observation room with me had their eyes trained on the fighting drama going on below. They were enjoying the fear and panic among the trapped Cathor army. Perhaps a bit too much. Now might be my chance. None could see me where I was concealed in that secret room above.

I saw the vile Koth, talking and laughing with his commanders watching with vicious glee the tragic deadly scene below them. Only Pondog stood close to me now, and he was also watching the Cathor army with an evil leer. I knew that now I had to make my escape. I was ready to put my plan into action. Somehow I had to quickly overcome Pondog and take his dagger and use it to break my chains.

It was at that moment, when I was shocked to see Lady Dallia brought into the room by two of Koth's black-robed warriors.

"Our scouts found her lurking outside the stronghold, master," one said as he flung her forward towards Koth.

"Ah, the lovely Dallia, come here to view the annihilation of the Cathor army? Or the death of Prince Tan, perhaps?" Koth spoke with a contemptuous sneer. "You shall rue your decision to defy my orders!"

Koth smiled evilly and he had her brought closer to him. Then he slapped her face.

She said nothing, standing tall and defiant.

"You filthy coward!" I shouted at seeing that treatment of my beloved. I grew livid with rage and swore that I would kill Koth before the next *tal* ended.

"Why have you come here? I told you to stay in Cathor!" Koth demanded full of anger.

"No! I will not!" she shouted back in defiant bravery. "I will not obey you any longer. I know who you are now, and I despise you and all you stand for. You will be defeated!"

Koth—the master of Zorr—totally vainglorious now, just continued to boast with grim laugher. As he did so, the defiant Dallia spit right into his grinning skull-like face.

"Good for you, Dallia!" I shouted laughing at Koth's embarrassment. The fact that I had noticed this and commented upon it enraged him even more.

Now Koth was burning red with anger and embarrassment at this insult from a mere woman. He clenched his fist and punched Dallia on the side of the head and in a moment my lovely lady lay motionless on the floor at my feet.

"She is a defiant little fool," Koth told me, trying to control his anger. "One more insult, and I swear she shall not live to be sent to Bamhor! Pondog, I am leaving now to begin the final destruction of the Cathor army. You stay here and watch them both. We shall deal with them later."

"Yes, master!" Pondog answered firmly.

Then Koth went to join his commanders as they left the room to continue their plans to deal with the trapped army below. I wondered what they had in store for the brave warriors of Cathor.

I could have rung Koth's throat with my bare hands and would have jumped at the chance to do so, but I was bound too well. I could barely move. Both my arms and legs were well chained to the wall, and I was pressed up against it rigidly. I thought to overcome Pondog and take his dagger to free myself, but I had to wait until he came close enough for me to do it. It did not appear that he would do so.

Meanwhile, my heart went out to Dallia, as she lay unconscious at my feet. That Koth could be so cruel I could not believe. If he hurt her further he would regret it. I would make him pay and pay well.

"Start the attack!" I heard Koth command with a loud bark. "Soon we shall cut to ribbons the last Cathor warrior and roast him over a fire during our victory feast!"

His generals and officers all cheered at this.

Below us I saw the large main door slowly opening. As it opened Cathor warriors both on foot, and still mounted, charged in an effort to force an escape, but to no avail. No sooner had the door been opened fully than two thousand of Koth's dark-robed and masked warriors entered and began their attack. I also saw another group of Cathors—traitors who rode under the banner of Len Le—who began to attack their own loyal fellows. This treasonous act made me sick with anger.

In no time hundreds of warriors lay dead while the loyal warriors of Cathor were surrounded by Len Le's treacherous host and Koth's army of outlaws.

At what price could Len Le do such a thing? He was a gifted general who had won many battles. He was trusted and an honorable man. Or so all thought. What had happened to him? Why should he turn traitor? What promise could Koth offer such a man to sway him to such evil?

Every man in that room with me was now fascinated by the battle going on below when I heard a tiny sound at my feet. It was Dallia, she was regaining consciousness. When she saw me, she hugged and kissed me joyfully. My heart leaped with joy that she was apparently uninjured. We were relieved to see that both of us were still alive and not hurt.

Pondog had long since moved forward to get a better view of the raging battle in the cavern below—or the slaughter—as it truly would soon become. Now that Dallia and I found ourselves alone, perhaps I could finally act.

I asked Dallia, "Where does that door lead to?" I was pointing to the doorway through which Dallia had been brought into the room.

"I think it is a storage room," she replied simply.

I nodded. "Is there some kind of passage there?"

"Yes, there is something at the far wall," she replied. "I saw it when I was dragged through the room. It is very narrow, and it leads downward into the Great Hall."

Now I had to ask Dallia something that was very important. She still had not gotten over the shock that her stepfather, Koth, was in fact the evil leader of these criminals and killers. That Koth was the so-called creature known as Zorr. She had always hated him, yet not even she could believe he could be such a horrid and depraved traitor.

I was still chained, and her hands were tied with a thick rope. Quietly she backed towards me, and I untied her hands and then whispered in her ear so that Pondog would not hear us. All the others were now too far away to notice us, being occupied watching the battle below. Pondog was my problem, he was closer to us—but he had the keys to my chains!

Dallia told me she had been thinking the same thing as she quietly sneaked up behind Pondog. Like all the others, his attention was transfixed upon the battle below for now it appeared the Cathors, though loosing the battle, were giving a good account of themselves. It had become a furious fight.

Unsuspected by Pondog, Dallia moved right behind him. I had untied her hands previously so that now she took a large stone which she unceremoniously let crash down upon the man's head. Pondog turned around in startled wonderment then slunk down to the floor into unconsciousness. Dallia holding his heavy bulk saw to it he was set down gently and quietly, so that the sound of his weapons and metal would not alert the others.

Noiselessly, Dallia took his sword and dagger, and then took the key to my chains and came back to me without a sound.

My heart raced as she came over to me with the key to my chains.

She was a wonderful woman, and could be a very dangerous one too.

"Quickly, unlock these chains!" I whispered and she immediately and very silently had me soon unbound, and then she placed Pondog's sword in my hand. She stood by with his dagger. I knew she knew how to use it. I smiled that we were finally free and now I could act. Now was our time!

The Zorrs had not noticed us yet. The battle below was going badly for the loyal Cathor troops as more and more of Koth's men filed into the trap. That upset the odds. I watched below in horror. I had to do something!

Now, with a sword in my hand we made our way cautiously behind Koth and his commanders, keeping myself between Dallia and the enemy. They had not noticed us yet. We were moving toward the doorway and soon would be out of the room. As luck would have it, at that very moment Koth suddenly turned around and he instantly took in the sight and realized right away what was happening.

"Get them!" Koth screamed in rage. "Do not let them escape!"

Soon I found myself facing half a dozen of Koth's officers. Swords were drawn, they gleamed silver and dark with dried blood. Battle began as I charged the group and instantly cut down two of the men. They were good swordsmen and had strength in numbers, but they had not reckoned with my rage and desire for revenge. It was great. I flew at them with a furious frenzy. I knew they had to be defeated and I would not allow them to win against me. For my fate, and for Dallia's. And for Rigel.

The enemy tried to surround me and cut us off from escaping the room. Koth shouted at them to fight on, but he stood always safely behind them. I protected Dallia as best I could, but she saw her opportunity and used her dagger to hamstring one of my attackers before he knew what was happening. The man went down in a scream of rage and pain. I finished him off and then moved on to the remaining three officers.

I fought with renewed fury, cutting and slashing a pattern of death and destruction to fight off my attackers and to keep Dallia safe. Just then a group of reinforcements came into the room, and she was dragged to the opposite wall.

"Good! Take her captive!" Koth demanded of his men in a guttural growl, "and now kill that Asudran!"

As Dallia struggled to escape from her captors, she called out to me pleadingly, "Tan, My Love! You must leave me! Go get help! Otherwise all is lost! Go now, do not worry, Koth will never kill me."

I could not leave my love, but I would not surrender to Koth again. I knew it meant instant death for me now—and eventually the same for Dallia. I knew I could not fight so many of the enemy and win to my beloved's side through combat in this place. I knew that she was right, as much as it galled me to admit it. I had to leave her and make my escape.

"Go now, my love!" Dallia urged one last time. "Escape! Quick! Before it is too late!"

"I will come back for you!" I shouted in a frenzied voice. "Have faith!"

"I do!" Dallia cried out.

I had little choice. Regretfully, I fought my way back to the door behind me. This was the same chamber in which Dallia had been brought into the observation room. I entered it. I now found myself in a smaller room, but with the door barred! The room though apparently only a storeroom seemed to have been built very strategically. I thought it was possibly built to be the last stronghold if the outer room was attacked and somehow overrun. That got me thinking. There must be some kind of secret passage out of here. There had to be! But where?

Dallia had told me that it was at the far wall and that it was a very narrow passageway, but all I saw there was a blank stone and rock wall.

Then I remembered the other secret door I had seen in the Great Hall below. That door was camouflaged and made of stone. It was almost invisible. This one could be designed the same way. Quickly, but cautiously, my fingers deftly swept the stone wall as the Zorr warriors outside pounded on the large heavy wooden door. Soon they would have it opened. I had to hurry.

I worked feverishly and soon found something that piqued my interest.

After what seemed a maddeningly long time, using what precious moments I had left, I found a secret panel and slid the concealed door open. Here I discovered a dimly lit narrow corridor and immediately I ran down into it as fast as I was able.

CHAPTER 15

After a long run I finally came to the end of the narrow corridor. Cautiously I opened another concealed lock, peaking inside this room I saw that it was empty and so I exited my passageway, and entered this new smaller room that led into another corridor. So far as I knew I had not been followed. Perhaps the guards were not able to find the secret passageway? I hoped that was true. I heard no sounds of pursuit as I looked up and down this new corridor, wondering where it would lead. Then I noticed a large metal door. This was the same type of door which I knew was blocking the Cathor army from the exit from their trap. The Cathors still were in a fight for their lives, I could hear them bravely battling and probably slowly being beaten. I knew I had to act fast if I was to save most of them.

Beside the door I found a small red button and sure of what it was, I immediately pressed it. Soon I was rewarded to see the large metal door slowly open upward with a loud grinding sound. Now I looked inside the Great Hall and was shocked to see the carnage within. The fight was devastating and still going on furiously.

"Quick!" I shouted getting the attention of the Cathor host, "Here! Over here! Cathors! Come this way to safety!"

Enough of them now saw me and heard my words so to change their direction and make for the opening I was pointing to. Now they saw a way to freedom out of this trap and all made for it. I continued to wave them onward.

At sight of this escape route the rest of the Cathor host took heart and fought like savages as they cut a path straight towards me and the opening to freedom. Their number had been drastically reduced, so that perhaps only half of the original five thousand troops remained. Those who remained were cut and bloody, many wounded, but all very brave and I could tell they still had a lot of fight left in them. As they valiantly showed. My heart fairly sang to see their bravery.

They rode steadfastly to where I beckoned at the opening. When all the survivors had fought their way out of the Great Hall, I hit that red button again, and with a resounding clang it lowered the large metal door shut. Shut tight. Trapping the Zorrs inside their own Great Hall in their own trap—and saving the Cathor army.

Some of the more belligerent Zorrs pressed on and had escaped the hall with the Cathors—but these few were soon easily and quickly dispatched. Now it was Koth's men who found themselves trapped. At least for the moment. They were cut off. So I knew I had to gather what remained of the Cathor host and make the most of the time we had to escape.

I mounted an unattended *ziba* and then called the Cathor warriors to me and ordered them to follow my lead. We were going to get out of this trap as fast as possible—and then perhaps—turn the tables on our enemy? Or so I hoped. Quickly we raced though the adjoining corridors until we reached the south exit of the enemy stronghold.

We rode on and met no large groups of Zorr warriors, only an occasional guard or two and they were quickly dispatched or rode away in panic. Soon though, we saw signs of pursuit as we heard the enemy riding swiftly up from behind us howling and cursing.

Riding the *ziba* of a fallen rider, with the portal open before us, we rode towards it. Soon our riders were pouring out of the enemy stronghold and rushing speedily through the foothills and woodlands of the Hills of Mystery.

A short time later we saw that about a thousand Zorr cavalry were pursuing us, but when we reached the flat plains away from the hills, they stopped the chase, for we were by then too far ahead for them to catch us.

We had escaped the Hills of Mystery and the enemy stronghold. I had miraculously come away from being Koth's prisoner a second time. Now I began to feel more optimistic, that my luck had finally changed for the better. Or so I thought. Those thoughts were also constantly on Dallia now as we raced southwards, and I feared for her plight.

What could I do now to stop Koth's mad rampage? I had no real plan. I spoke with the Cathor survivors, all brave men, but many of them wanted to go back to Cathor. I held them together forcefully as we neared the Glittering City of Jewels where we found ourselves suddenly attacked by Cathor troops coming out from the city.

"What is this?" one of my men asked me aghast.

We had taken small losses so far, but I realized we could expect no aid from Cathor now, for the city was obviously under Koth's control.

"The city has fallen to the enemy in our absence," I told the men as they gathered around me. "It was Koth's plan all along, he is the man behind the mask of Zorr."

"Traitor!" some of my men yelled full of anger.

Then I explained what I knew of this to them. I told them what Koth and his Zorr fiends were up to.

My men shouted out, "Traitors! Traitors! Kill them all!"

I nodded, then spoke up. "We must continue the fight! And we will win! Traitors will get their due!"

The Cathor troops cheered my words. I tightened my jaw and hoped that their words would not just prove to be merely bold words.

I thought of the old emperor of Cathor. He would never have ordered this attack. Probably old Kartor lay dead by now. But whether he lay dead or not, I knew we could not expect any help from Cathor.

So once again a huge group of Cathor warriors and I found ourselves fleeing from warriors from their own city. Where would we go? I did not know for now. Now it seemed, *we* had become the outlaws!

I decided that our best course now would be to go to my home city of Asudra, Koths agents did not rule there. My uncle ruled and was a powerful emperor, but there was a problem. The distance and the time to get there, which I knew placed Dallia in peril. I needed another plan. Since the Zorrs ruled in Vorba, that city was out. Bamhor was an unfriendly country, especially to Dallia and me. So where to go? I decided the only city we might expect aid from was my own city, Asudra. However, Asudra was so far away, far south and east in direction. It would take many *talas* for us to get there, assemble a force of warriors, and then come back to Cathor. It was a tricky business, but it seemed the only alternative to defeat Koth and his forces. Meanwhile, what of Dallia's fate? I had to save her.

That night when we camped, there were almost two thousand of the brave Cathors who were left, some of the badly wounded had died in our encounter with the troops sent to attack us from Cathor. We ate and slept and licked our wounds. We spoke of the best plan to stop Koth and everyone agreed, once I explained the situation to them, that we must make for Asudra.

With daylight we mounted up and headed south for Asudra. Dallia was constantly on my mind now, as I rode silently immersed in my own thoughts. How was she doing? What had happened to her? Had she already been sent to Bamhor and its vile emperor for marrage? These were some of the fearsome thoughts going on in my mind when I became frantic, for I realized soon would come the time Dallia was to leave to become the mate of Selek of Bamhor!

I hardly had the presence of mind to think about this. What could I do? It gnawed at my insides. What could I do to save her? I decided I must go to Bamhor. It was then that my attention was taken by one of our scouts who warned that a large group of what looked to be thousands of warriors was riding up behind us.

"They must be Zorrs," the scout told me as he rode up beside my mount.

I was not so sure, but I spoke the order, "Make haste!"

I led my warriors to ride hard to the left, racing away from the Zorrs and towards the city of Bamhor where Dallia would be. Here at least I hoped to intercept her caravan and save her before she entered the city and took that final wasteful act of defiance to destroy herself rather than be placed into the arms of an enemy. I must save her before she took that dreadful alternative.

As I turned my force of riders, I noticed that the large group of warriors kept following us. It seemed they also turned their direction trying to flank our escape.

After some time, they were much closer, bearing down upon us hard. I noticed as they got close to us that the traitors Len Le and Pondog were in the lead of this large force of warriors. I grew enraged at the sight of then, but we could not be stopped now. I had my men spur their mounts and soon we outdistanced them as our mounts were more rested than their own. It simply came down to that. So now, for the moment, we were safe from them. Obviously, they had been riding hard all day and night to catch up with us.

We were riding with them behind us for many *tals*, and always we kept our lead on our enemy no matter how hard they tried to catch up with us. We could stay ahead of them—for now. We were outnumbered by two to one but were safe as long as we could keep our pace and hold our lead over our enemy.

We raced east towards Bamhor, for I had my Lady Dallia always upon my mind. Soon we spotted more movement south of us proceeded by a gigantic cloud of dust.

"More riders!" an officer told me, calling my attention to an enormous dust cloud.

I had already seen it and could tell that it must be a huge horde of riders to make such a massive cloud.

"We are being followed also from the south now." I noticed to the officer.

"They are surely riders and there must be many thousands of them," one of my men added.

I nodded; my officer seemed correct. I wondered who they might be? They could not be Zorrs, not coming from that direction. They must be from Vorba, for by now we were closer to that powerful city. If they were warriors from Vorba we could expect no help from them, for that city was also known to be under Koth's control.

We had been racing across the great plains of Rigel for the entire *tala* in an effort to escape our Zorr pursuers and reach the city of Bamhor. There were only a few hours of sun light left to us, yet we were still almost a full one *tala* journey from our destination. It all seemed so hopeless, but I would never despair—nor would I give up without a fight.

Soon one group of our pursuers, either Koth's men, or his Vorba allies, must catch up to us. Then we would be caught in a two-prong trap. I knew we could not run forever for our *zibas* were getting tired and would soon be exhausted. So were my men. Most Cathor warriors, as strong, bold and agile as were their weapons, but they were not used to running away from their enemies. Nor running away from a fight. Nevertheless, we pressed our ponderous mounts onward, even as they began to tire and weaken. Some of the huge beasts eventually dropped dead of exhaustion. The riders being furiously thrown, or dragged, some of them died, others were injured. Some were even trampled by their own floundering beast. We could not afford to stop to save these riders, but I ordered men to ride back and quickly lift the survivors upon the back of their own mount. It was a grizzly race of life and death.

It seemed there was no way out of this predicament other than stop and fight what must become a losing battle with our Zorr antagonists. Then I found just what I was looking for, a small hilly area. It would make a perfect defendable spot and would be a severe disadvantage for our enemy to come against us, with us on high ground. This seemed our only hope.

I ordered my men to change course and we approached the hills in front of us. I looked back and saw what looked like a triumphant leer on the faces of Len Le and Pondog. No sooner did we race up the hilltops—which was a fairly steep ride on our *zibas* being large flat plains animals—we were being surrounded by our Zorr enemies. My men were set and ready. The enemy attack began immediately. Len Le and Pondog and some officers looked on in safety as their men did the dirty work. They came at us in a rapid charge. The battle began in a wild clash. It went on furiously and my men fought bravely. We would at least go down fighting and bring many Zorrs with us to their doom—as well as our own.

My mount turned suddenly as I saw the enemy come up behind me. There were three of them, riding abreast, coming at me with bloodied swords. Instantly I was all action and raced upon them with sword swinging in long deadly arcs. At the last instant I turned my mount outflanking their charge, and from the outside met the man at the far right of the trio. I came at him hard and fast. My sword sung a song of blood past his guard and imbedded itself into his chest. My blade ran in deep. It was all over for him immediately. He dropped down dead from his mount instantly.

I now turned my mount and charged down at the remaining two enemy warriors. I had put one down quickly and then swerved my mount to meet the last rider head-on. He now had finally turned his zibas so we faced each other, but off to my side I noticed another attacker had come upon me. This newer opponent was coming at me from behind. I had to do some wild riding and swift swordsmanship to fight off this threat. In the end I was able to dispatch both these men quickly. I had since discovered that many of these Zorrs were not very good swordsmen, only very deadly when attacking innocent women and children. Or unarmed civilians. Then they felt bold and blustery. I spit upon them.

I saw that my men were fighting the enemy furiously, taking down thrice the toll of Zorr warriors. Everywhere there was blood, death and screams of pain mingled with hoary oaths. The battlefield had become a charnel house.

Finally I saw the traitorous Cathor general, Len Le, and my anger burned furiously. Never was I so enraged to see any man. He and his officers were former comrades and friends of my men and now were their most hated enemies. And my own! I wanted them all dead! I made a dead-end mounted charge at Len Le, but he would not confront me and quickly he and his minions withdrew a safe distance from me and my men. How brave of him!

"The Master Zorr," Len Le shouted now as he had his men move forward towards me, "wishes to have you taken alive, if possible. Surrender and spare the needless deaths of you and your men. Come forward to us and lay down your weapons."

I looked at my men to see how many would go over to Len Le as prisoners. Not one of them moved forward, all still held their swords menacingly. Waiting for battle. I felt the joy of the warrior as I saw them. The pride of their bravery and loyalty touched my heart.

"We will not submit!" I shouted in a loud voice so that all my men could hear me.

I would never submit to the ghastly torture that I knew awaited me if I should ever fall into Koth's hands again. Len Le was waiting impatiently, but not one of my men moved. To a man they had decided to stay and fight, to sell their lives dearly. The battle had cost us much in death and injures, but we were not done yet.

"We will not submit!" I shouted, and my men repeated my words in a loud growl.

I looked at my men, those that were left. There were perhaps a few hundred or so of those remaining. Len Le's force easily was ten times our number. I nodded, so be it. We all laughed with a shrug at Len Le's demand, then his men moved forward with the order to wipe us out.

"Kill them all!" Len Le ordered his men as they slowly and carefully rode forward upon us. We were ready for them and willing to fight to the death against them. We were very dangerous, and they were very wary of our bloody blades.

"We will never submit!" I shouted the order to my men, "Charge!"

Len Le shouted back, "Fools! Mighty Zorr will have the head of each of you slime to decorate the arches of the Florian Palace!"

I nodded, smiled grimly, "Then come and get us!"

We charged the enemy host in a wild attack that sprawled into a uncontrollable melee. It was incredible and bloody and my men fought like the champions they were. As I fought, my mind could not help but dwell upon thoughts that now I would never see my beloved Dallia again. I knew what the outcome of this battle must be—the odds were very much against us winning through. I revolted at the thought of Dallia destroying herself, but perhaps it was better than struggling in the arms of that monster Selek of Bamhor. Though knowing my Dallia, if she had the opportunity, she might slip a slim dagger into his putrid heart. At least I hoped she might have that opportunity.

My thoughts of my beloved were broken as Len Le's traitors were once again riding upon the rise of a wide hill. Instantly we were all pressed by them, but determined to kill as many of the enemy as we could. We knew this was probably the end for us, so we fought all the harder. A large number of Zorr warriors went down in the initial attack before they knew what had hit them. My men fought bravely and with a zeal never seen before by the warriors of Rigel. Rigel was truly a warrior world.

All about us lay a large pile of the enemy dead and their huge mounts, mixed with too many of my own valiant warriors who had also fallen. They lay in great heaps higher than a tall man's head in some places. This attested to the intensity of the battle in certain places. It was as if they formed a wall around us, and that gave me an idea. We continued to fight furiously, but somehow for now we held the enemy at bay.

It seemed, in fact, we were doing almost too well. I put that to the poor swordsmanship of our attackers and the fine fighting ability of the trained warriors of Cathor under my command. Only the best of my fighters were left now. Hardy fellows who would not be taken down easily—only at a high cost in enemy lives.

By now there were barely a hundred of my brave fellows left alive, the best warriors of Cathor to be sure—loyal and true every one of them. They cut down row upon row of attacking Zorrs. The thought that my small force of about one hundred men could do this much damage to Len Le's army was angrily written into his face. His men were now beginning to become wary of attacking us, our furious counterattacks were causing them much damage and for some to move away in fear. I had just enough men to ring the top of our small hill, so that the enemy could not get to our rear. We fought side by side, each man backing up

"CHARGE!"

the other, so there was no way we could be flanked for now.

As one of our warriors occasionally went down to a blade or axe, no sooner did his body hit the ground than another brave man took his place, a bloody sword in his ever ready hand.

Even with their superior numbers the enemy could not get through our line to overrun our position. My remaining warriors were superior to any of their attackers and proved it to them over and over—so much so that the attackers did not press us hard any longer, and many even backed off in abject fear.

Seeing this my men and I gave out a lusty cheer and began to get some measure of renewed hope which only spurred us to fight ever harder. We knew we could not win, but we surely were giving a good account of ourselves, surely a battle that would be sung loudly around the fires of our people. Then I noticed the other group of Vorba troops riding quickly towards us. They were close now. My heart sank to see so many of them. They were riding hard to catch up to us. There must have been twenty thousand of them, a massive horde, more than I had ever thought there were earlier. The very ground shook with the weight of their monstrous raging mounts at full charge. They were still too far away however for me to pick out any details of individuals.

We could do nothing about that now, we just had to fight on to our doom while the reinforcements were on their way to aid our attackers. It was a most disheartening sight.

CHAPTER 16

We fought on furiously like the mythological heroes of ancient Rigel, but seemingly without any hope. Even if by some miracle we defeated Len Le's force, there were still at least twenty thousand warriors riding hard and fast towards us from the south. Who were they? We had no idea. However, we feared they were warriors out of Vorba, and as such that meant they were allies of Koth and the Zorrs. Enemies! Sure defeat!

As this new threat came close enough for us to see them more clearly our hearts sank for they were indeed warriors from out of Vorba. We could now see plainly by their banners, their fighting harness, red cloaks, black feathered helmets and their bold colors set for war. It was a massive enemy force.

As they approached us, Len Le and his men showed expressions of delight and boisterous victory, cheering and shouting with bold words. The Vorba horde came closer and were soon near the hill my men were still holding. Len Le rode with Pondog and a few others to speak with the Vorba commander, while I and my men were determined to fight and die upon that hill —- and take as many of Len Le's traitorous Cathor warriors with us into the darkest depths of Ibar's bleak underworld.

My men and I kept fighting the enemy, showing them how noble warriors fought and died in battle. We all knew the final outcome for us, a quick death or torture, but now we realized that outcome would happen very soon indeed. So be it!

I noticed the Vorba commander and Len Le had been talking together perhaps a few moments when I saw Len Le and Pondog and their men move off, and instantly they were surrounded—and then they were attacked! I was astonished by this turn of events. What could that be about? I was shocked and my men and I watched with amazement, as our attackers also stopped fighting to see what was going on. There was a strange lull in our battle. We watched with surprise to see a new battle rage on among the newcomers from Vorba, and soon Len Le, Pondog and the members of his party surrendered. They were quickly bound, disarmed and now prisoners of the Vorba horde. All this had transpired in the blink of an eye. I hardly knew what to make of it.

I could not grasp the full meaning of what I had just seen, when suddenly a large hairy enemy brute just missed chopping my arm off. I admit I had been distracted by what I had seen happening with the Vorba warriors, when that brute Zorr came after me. I was surprised by the force of his attack but I regained my balance quickly. We had a brief but hard fought battle and then my sword blade slashed his face, and while he was screaming in pain, my sword point found his heart. When I had dispatched this antagonist I was free once again to look down and see what the Vorbas were up to.

I was astounded to see the Vorbas quickly surrounding the bottom of our hill, enclosing us and the Zorrs in a nice tight trap—but for what reason I could not guess. Men of Len Le's army and my own warriors looked on in utter surprise and wonder. Neither of our forces knew what was happening.

It was at that moment when the Vorba force suddenly moved into position and attacked the Zorr rear. It was astonishing. Our enemy now found themselves surrounded and outnumbered, shocked by the attack of this new force they thought to be allies—who were in fact their enemies. Without their leader Len-Le, they lost direction and heart and began to try to flee or surrender.

It was then I noticed the man commanding the Vorba force. While I had never seen him before, I did know the younger man that rode at his side. I was happy to see that it was none other than my friend Droth Zel, and that he had somehow arrived with help just in time. A lot of help! I was ecstatic and my men cheered when I told them that the Vorba warriors were our allies.

That night we made camp and licked our wounds as we spoke with our new allies. All the Zorrs and their Cathor traitor allies, were now prisoners securely bound and guarded. They would be no more trouble. Len Le was also held and would be tried back in Cathor for treason.

Soon the Vorba commander, with Droth Zel and myself were able to talk for the first time after the battle. As you can imagine I had many questions. Droth and I greeted each other warmly, especially since we each supposed the other was dead or captured.

"Prince Tan Alvaka," Droth Zel introduced me formally indicating the commander of the Vorba host, "I have the honor to present to you Ven Og, emperor of Vorba."

I smiled and bowed, "I thank you greatly for your assistance and timely arrival," I told him, then added, "How is it that Vorba is not under the control of Koth and his Zorr creatures?"

"Koth?" both men said curiously. "Who is Koth?"

"He is better known as the leader of the Zorrs," I told them in a sure tone. "Koth, First Minister of Cathor, is now, from what I have discovered, the secret leader of the Zorrs."

Both Droth Zel and Ven Og were shocked by this news.

"How do you know that this Koth of Cathor is secretly the leader of these fiends? He is high in the structure of Cathor," Droth asked. "How do you know this?"

Then I told them what had befallen me since Droth and I had separated. It was a long story and they asked many questions. Both Droth and Ven were visibly impressed.

"Then that makes our job so much easier," Ven spoke up happily. "Now that we know who the enemy leader is, and fully understand the Zorr menace, we can deal with them most effectively."

"Now I have some questions for you," I asked curiously. "What happened in Vorba? How is it that you and your city are free of the Zorr yoke?"

"To make a long story short," Droth said with a slim smile, "when I left you I went to Vorba as planned. There I was imprisoned with an ex-prince of Vorba. That was this man, Ven Og, son of Kox Og, emperor of Vorba."

"Both Ven Og and myself decided to work together to escape," Droth told me. "We were on the same side so we made our plans until finally we were able to escape the prison and flee the city to the south, to your native city of Asudra, Tan. When we got there we found the city mobilized for war, and near ready to move against Cathor. We spoke to your uncle, Azare Alvaka, the emperor of the city. We alerted him to the Zorr threat, which he knew about only too well. It seems that there had been recent attempts on his life by their agents, obviously none had succeeded."

I looked at Ven fearfully. "Is my uncle all right?"

"He is fine," Ven replied with a smile. Then he continued, "The would-be assassins were caught and were made to tell all they knew. They told an interesting story and gave up much valuable information."

"My uncle is a stern man who brooks no foolishness," I stated seriously.

"Indeed!" Ven replied, with a short nod of his head. "Because of this he called out all his troops in a great army. There were fifty thousand Asudra warriors and another twenty thousand Bovars, and they moved north with us to retake Vorba from our enemies. The city fell to us almost immediately. They had no taste for what we were serving."

"The city was taken quickly and Ven Og remained behind to organize the new government. Meanwhile Azare, with his combined army of some seventy thousand warriors moved north to Aboola, that stronghold city of the Zorrs, and that is the last we heard of them."

"That is good to hear," I said, trying to understand all that this now meant.

Then Droth continued, "When we met you we were on our way to join the Asudra and Bovar combined army to seige Cathor. However, once we noticed your two groups of Cathor warriors that seemed to be at odds against each other—one chasing the other over the plains—we grew naturally curious and decided to see what that was about. When we saw the large group attacking the smaller one, we knew something was wrong. Once we caught up to you it was then that Len Le rode up to meet us—see he thought we were loyal to Zorr—so we soon knew that he and his men were traitors and our true enemy."

"How could you tell so quickly?" I asked in surprise.

Droth smiled slyly, "He demanded to see the Gold Ring wearer who was in command of our force."

"Ah!" I smiled knowingly.

"Exactly," Ven added with a growl. "You can not imagine how angry that made me. I was the man in command, not some traitorous Zorr ring wearing fiend."

We talked a long time that night. We had decided to send a small group of warriors south to nearby Vorba with the Zorr prisoners and all the wounded.

Len Le, Pondog and these traitors would be returned to Cathor for punishment.

The rest of our force would ride north to the aid of Aboola, to free that city and it's people from Koth's death grip. It was believed better to rest our army for the night and then get an early start the next morning and race to Aboola.

Then we slept, and I hit sweet slumber quickly and deeply, yet I could not sleep for very long. Terrible thoughts and doubts haunted my mind. While in my dreams there was now hope that I might see Dallia again. I had a nagging fear that she might be with Selek of Bamhor at that very moment. Then what? I knew what that meant. Dallia would take her own life! My mind reeled at the realization.

When I had spoken of this to Droth, he promised me he would send a messenger to the court of Selek. It seemed, temporarily at least, Selek had become our ally. He was ever a most nervous leader who bent with every wisp of the political winds. Immediately the messengers were given their orders and raced out of our camp upon their freshly rested *zibas*. I now felt somewhat relieved about our situation concerning Dallia's safety, so I was able to doze off to a long awaited restful sleep.

CHAPTER 17

Early the next morning we raced northward to Aboola. It was there I hoped that by making good time, we would meet Azare and his ally army. Our race north was uneventful so that one *tala* later we spotted the red spires and turrets of distant Aboola. I feared for Dallia as I knew time was running out for her.

As we neared the large city, Ven og, Droth Zel and I, approached the great wall with a small group of warriors. Instantly the huge gate opened and a company of riders came out to meet us. They were warriors and came at us rapidly. They were armed and armored. I wondered who they were and what their game might be. I smiled gravely. I knew I would find out soon enough. As the riders came closer my heart soon leapt with joy, for I noticed that in their van were two men I instantly recognized, my friends Onat and Saad.

"Tan Alvaka! And you have brought an army with you! That is good! It is good to see you again, my friend," Onat told me as his companion Saad nodded agreement. "The emperor shall be riding out to meet you personally."

"Selek?" I asked curiously, for I did not see him as being friendly towards us at all. He had proved to be a most dubious ally.

Saad smiled, "You shall see, Tan."

I looked at him curiously, "Tell me, my friend, what of Dallia?"

"I am sorry, Tan." Droth spoke up sadly. He had heard from his riders with news that was not good.

"She is not…dead?" I asked him in a crackling voice.

"No! No not that!" Droth spoke up quickly, "We just do not know what befell her. Or her whereabouts."

Onat added, "We searched but we did not find her here in the city."

Droth spoke up softly to me, "Keep hope."

I nodded, but my fears for her were swirling within my troubled mind.

"Any other questions?" Droth asked me.

I signed deeply, "Well, then tell me, what has happened to the Zorr warriors who I thought controlled this city? And where is the Ausdra and Bovar army?"

Onat looked at me and stated with a wide grin, "Azare has already been here with both armies. The Zorrs took one look at his massive host and they fled leaving the city. I told Azare, your uncle, that the last time I saw you alive, you were in Cathor. So after the battle was done here, he left with his army to go to that city. To free Cathor—and to find you."

"Reports tell us," Saad added, "that Cathor is under a heavy siege. Azare needs the Vorba troops there to join him and help turn the tide in his favor."

"Then that is what we shall do. Now that things seem to be settled here, we shall ride for Cathor immediately," Droth Zel spoke up. "Do you think that Aboola can aid us with any of it's warriors?"

"You must talk with our emperor on such an important matter," Saad replied, then he pointed to the city gate. "Here he comes now."

Then out from the city under heavy guard and surrounded by officers, officials and ministers was the emperor of Aboola. It was a great surprise for it was none other than my friend, Beeg. I had no clue that he was a noble, he certainly did not act like one. He was now the ruler of Aboola, since his father had been slain by the Zorrs because he would not cooperate and follow their orders.

To say I was surprised would be a massive understatement. It was good to see my friend alive, and now that he had regained the throne of his beloved city, we had another strong ally in our fight.

As the two groups came together, we greeted each other warmly. Soon emperor, Beeg Alon—to give him his full name and title—with his friends, Saad and Onat at his side, along with twenty thousand Aboola warriors, and myself, rode off together to break the siege of Cathor.

As we rode on I spoke with Beeg and he told me that Droth's bother, and my friend, Hotath Zel, was alive and well with Azare's army. As we left for Cathor I had the hope of seeing Dallia once more also, as well as seeing my uncle Azare and Hotath once again.

We rode on at a swift pace. Our ponderous *ziba* mounts thundering over the flat grassy plains of Rigel. As I rode I always had in my mind thoughts of my beloved Dallia. I was in a better mood when one of the messengers Droth had sent to Bamhor returned telling me that Dallia seemed to be nowhere in that city—that she had apparently not yet arrived. That was good. But where was she?

I thought that over. Obviously, Koth's plans had been so upset by the fall of Vorba and Aboola that he had not the time or men to send Dallia to Selek in Bamhor. Or so I surmised. What else could it be? I hoped she was still safe at home in Cathor. I knew I would find out soon enough.

Whatever the reason, Dallia was not in the city of Bamhor, so she was safe from Selek, but where she was and in what manner of health I did not yet know. It plagued me deeply.

That night after riding hard all day we camped again, made our plans, and early the next morning started out to Cathor. By mid-afternoon we reached Cathor, known as The Glittering City of Jewels. We were not alone. For we could see that the city was under siege from a mighty army. Surrounding Cathor were some seventy thousand Asudra and Bovar warriors who were encamped closing off the city. Cathor was completely under siege now. As our force approached, outriders came out to meet us and direct us to Arazre's headquarters tent. So leaving our men, Ven Og, Droth Zel, Saad, Onat, Beeg Alon, and I rode to the headquarters of my uncle in the Asudra main camp.

CHAPTER 18

Once in the Asudra camp we were ushered into a large elaborate tent. It was fit for an emperor of a great city. Here I saw Azare, my uncle who was the emperor of Asurda, along with old friends Hotath Zel, Captain Soth and Hupa. I greeted my uncle warmly and then greeted Hotath with good cheer. I was relieved to see all were well and alive after so much time and so many travails.

The two brothers, Droth and Hotath left us soon for they had much to talk about and catch up on. They had not seen each other for a very long while.

As I looked upon Soth and Hupa I smiled, for I could not help rejoicing that they had gotten through to Asudra and enlisted our army in our cause. We all talked and laughed for quite a while as we each told our stories. We were happy now since it appeared we would be victorious against Koth and the Zorrs. I scoffed at the fellow's very name now. However Koth and his minions were still a very viable threat. With all the greetings and talk over with, we settled down to the serious business of winning the siege of Cathor.

Our main objective of course was to enter Cathor, capture Koth if possible, and destroy this secret society of black-robed and masked killers. My main objective was to find Dallia as soon as possible and come to her aid. I constantly worried about her and wondered what had happened to her.

"What is this stronghold I have heard so much about?" Azare asked me as he gave a contemptuous sneer at the besieged city. He was confident it would fall soon to his army. "I fear we must also send troops there and clean out that nest of vermin if we are ever to truly defeat these Zorr killers. They must be stopped. None of them must be left alive. Where is this place, Tan? Ven Og? Do you know?"

Ven Og did not know and said so, but I spoke up, "I know it very well. It is secreted in the Hills of Mystery to the north. I can lead a force there if need be."

"That is good, Tan. Then you shall do so," Azare told me with a sure nod of his head and a regal smile.

"It is very strongly protected," Droth Zel added.

"Well, that is another problem," Azare said thoughtfully. "We must keep the siege here until Cathor falls. I am sure the people inside the city are with us, but their army has been co-opted by these villains and criminals."

"And by Koth, who is the First Minister of the city and the real hand behind the emperor—if in fact old Kartor still lives at all," I spoke up.

"Then we must also conqueror this stronghold of the Zorrs. They must have no place to run or hide when the battle here is over."

I volunteered to lead a force north and attack the Zorr stronghold, for I believed that Koth would most probably be hiding there—and with him would surely be my beloved Dallia. I doubted Koth would be in Cathor now, a slippery *squal*-like him would have left the city before the siege closed it off and made escape impossible. I knew his kind. However, at the stronghold he would have a much better advantage from capture. He could also regroup his forces, which was a prime concern for me.

"Cathor is weak and the city will fall soon," I told the allied leaders and there was agreement all around. "Koth's twisted vision of empire is falling apart before his eyes. However, he is more dangerous now than ever. Koth must be holed up in the Zorr stronghold to the north. We must hurry otherwise he will escape us. I have seen him and spoken with him. We can never allow this man to escape us. If he does escape, none of our lives, or the lives of our friends and families, will ever be safe."

"You think he will come after us and our families personally?" Azare asked me.

"Absolutely," I replied surely.

My words had a most sobering effect upon everyone there.

"He sounds like he must be some kind of mad man," Beeg added.

"He is mad," I spoke up, "but one with a madness ruled by a powerful intelligence and a vile wickedness. He has a way of controlling people and convincing them to his cause. It is almost uncanny. He has some kind of power over men and their minds."

"Then we must stop him," Azare spoke up firmly.

"What do you need to stop him, Tan?" Ven Og asked me.

"Give me a hundred warriors on swift *zibas*, and I shall leave immediately for their stronghold," I told him and soon my request was granted.

I knew that most of Koth's forces came from Cathor and most were fighting in the defense of their city. They had been lied to and misled, of course, but the die was cast now. War and siege were the only result. I also knew that the majority of the people of Cathor were in revolt against the Zorrs so that Koth's forces found themselves fighting off the siege and many of the citizens of the city they had oppressed for so long.

Soon I had gathered my men, all of whom were brave Asudra warriors from my city and they were led by my friend Captain Soth. Then we mounted our ponderous *zibas* and charged across the endless plains of Rigel northwards to the Zorr stronghold. We left Cathor far behind us, but were sure that soon the siege would force that city to surrender. Then those warriors could join us. For now it was paramount for me to capture—or kill—Koth. I would do so with relish.

We had ridden all day and still had seen no sight of any Zorr patrols that so recently had controlled all the lands around the Hills of Mystery and southwards to the Great River. Even the warlike Zunds, who inhabited the land had moved westward when the Zorrs, who they greatly feared, had begun to occupy the territory.

It was not long before we were in the Hills of Mystery, continually looking for sentries or patrols, hidden traps, and ambushes. This time no matter how hard we looked we saw none of the enemy. It seemed most strange. I wondered where they had all gone to. They seemed to be nowhere in sight. I knew all of them were not in the battle lines at Cathor. So where could they be?

"It appears they have all fled the territory," Captain Soth told me. "There is no one in this area at all."

"Perhaps, but we must be ever vigilant," I told him and that was just what we proceeded to do.

We rode on and finally came to the southern entrance to the enemy stronghold. It appeared to be unguarded. Here it was quiet and empty. We entered most warily, dismounted, and then walked our mounts down the long corridor to the stables. Inside we found about a dozen *zibas*, also untended and unguarded.

I looked at Soth but he just shrugged.

"There are a dozen *zibas* here, so there must be at least a dozen men here as well. Somewhere," I told Soth and my men. "Caution yourselves."

We continued onward deeper into the massive structure. If there were in fact a dozen enemy warriors here, as the number of mounts seemed to indicate, I hoped Dallia would be among them. Also Koth. We were making our way towards the Great Hall. So far we had seen none of the enemy. The place appeared to be deserted. I could not believe that, so I impressed upon my men to be very wary of a trap. Remembering the entrapment of the Cathor army I stood by the large arched doorway and looked into the Great Hall. I was astounded by what I saw.

All throughout the immense area of the Great Hall it was littered with the dead bodies of Zorr and Cathor warriors. My eyes scanned the area above the hall to the ceiling and then my eyes found the secret room in which Dallia had been imprisoned by Koth. It all seemed so long ago now. I could see that the secret door built into the stone wall was open and I made my way towards that location. My men fanned out, examining everything and astounded by what they found. I walked cautiously upwards over the bodies of many dead men, Koth's men, still dressed in black robes and wearing their horrid deformed face masks. They were all dead. When I reached the great chamber above, I found it empty. My heart sank. There was no sight of Koth, or of Dallia, nor any of his men alive anywhere. Where were they?

I sent parties of men in small groups of five to search all sections of that gargantuan labyrinthine underground fortress. It took some time because the place was so intricately massive. When we all met to report what we had found, none of us had seen any of the enemy, only the dead. They were everywhere. I was most perplexed.

It was later when we were all together in a here-to-for unexplored section of the stronghold that we came to the Pit of the Dead. My old prison. Here it was that Droth and I had previously been imprisoned and cruelly baited by the commander of the stronghold. I would like to meet that fellow once more also, but this time with a sword in my hand to do a bit of productive carving.

"So where is everyone?" I asked curiously. I looked at my men and could see that they were thinking the same thing.

Then we heard a sudden noise, such as a man coughing. I tensed and immediately looked below down into the Pit of the Dead.

"There is someone down there!" Captain Soth cried out in surprise as we all ran over to the rim of the pit. The door was open, and we could look down within.

Cautiously we examined the pit and what lay within one hundred *haads* far below.

"There are five men down there," I shouted. "Quickly we need to get them out!"

Immediately I sent two of my men with a rope to go down into the pit and bring up the prisoners. There were five of them and later we found out there were other larger cells with many dozens of other prisoners. They were starved and haggard, but thankful and much relieved.

"Who are you?" I asked the man who I assumed to be their leader.

"I am called Abu Zel," said the man who though worn and starved, I could see was a distinguished white-haired nobleman. "Me, and the members of my clan, have been trapped here for many days. Who are you?"

I smiled. The leader of the Zel clan! Then we talked.

He was indeed Abu Zel, the long lost father of Droth and Hotath. I told him both his sons were alive and well and even now serving at the siege of Cathor. He had not seen his sons for a very long time and when he learned they were safe a big smile crossed his haggard face.

Altogether we were able to rescue almost a hundred people from those terrible prison pits, most of them were older men and women who because of their age could not actively join the Tog movement to fight the Zorr threat. They had been hiding in the Hills of Mystery for a long time where they were found and imprisoned by Koth.

"Have any of you recently seen Koth, the leader of the Zorrs?" I asked Abu and his people.

"Yes, but we do not know anything of his movements," Abu explained. "He goes about robed and masked at all times."

"So he was here and we missed him?" I asked impatiently.

"I am not certain. Where he and his men may be is anyone's guess," Abu replied.

"Did you see a lovely young woman with him? Dallia of Cathor," I asked hopefully.

"No, sorry, we were kept imprisoned and I was only brought to the presence of the leader when he called me to insult and threaten me and my clan members if we did not join him. He seemed to want to have the support of my clan in his activities. We would not!" Abu said softly, but with pride.

As time passed a little more searching convinced us the stronghold had been abandoned by Koth and his men. I thought it most strange, but that seemed to be true.

Afterwards that night I posted guards all around as we slept in the Great Hall in a cleared area where the dead had been removed. The stench of death and decay was still strong there but we had to deal with it for that one night. I did not want to leave the place just yet. I felt there was something we were missing here. I had no way to explain it, but it was a feeling I had that I have learned over time that I must listen to.

We all slept in the Great Hall after we gave our starving allies what food and water we had to share. The Zels were very grateful. They had taken on a big job and it appeared now that they would win their fight, but they had paid a dear price for victory. Out of some five hundred people who had originally went to hide in the hills, now only these eighty-two were left alive, all others had been killed or tortured to death by Koth, or the stronghold commander. I had great respect for Abu Zel and the four others who had been imprisoned with him in the Pit of the Dead, for I also had been a reluctant guest there and gone through the agony of it.

It was hours later in the middle of the night, and it was deathly quiet, but I could have sworn that I had heard a strange sound. I saw my guards were still on duty at the far side of the chamber and all seemed well, but still I sensed something was wrong.

Was it some aspect of my over-active imagination? Was it fear for the safety of Dallia? I still had not found her and had no idea where she might be. It was burning my heart and twisting my mind. I lay my head back down, but could not sleep.

I looked around me. Everyone in my party, and all of the Zels were in a deep slumber, but as I stood up I noticed Abu Zel staring at me most carefully.

"Did you hear it?" he asked me in a silent ominous whisper.

"I do not know what I heard," I told him.

"Well, I heard something," he told me.

"Come, let us see what it is," I replied softly and in a heartbeat we were up with drawn swords out and ready.

Everyone else was apparently well asleep, with the deep slumber of the exhausted. And we saw no reason to wake them. They all needed their rest and strength for the morning's travel. Slowly and quietly Abu and I neared the end of the massive chamber. Then we heard the noise once again. It was the sound a sword makes scraping stone. It had come from behind us deep inside the stronghold. Probably from the lower abandoned tunnels. Or were they abandoned? I began to wonder. I know I had sent men down there to search the depths, and they had reported that it did not seem worth it to search deeper. I had accepted their report. Now I feared I may have made a grave error. Well, perhaps I had? Or perhaps not? I could not be sure and did not want to take any more chances now. I looked at Abu and he nodded and followed me. My nerves tensed as we noticed that only one of my men was now standing there on guard. Where was the other guard? Now Abu and I were alert that something was not right, fearful of some kind of trap.

As we walked across the huge chamber, I looked for the missing guard. The remaining guard pointed to one of the corridors.

I called out the missing guard's name in a soft voice. "Sovan?" I asked once more, "Sovan? Where are you?"

There was no reply. A fierce chill ran through me.

I whispered his name louder until we came to the opening of the corridor. "Where are you, Sovan?"

Abu and I, with the remaining guard, had received our answer very soon when we came upon Sovan's bloody body at the corner of an intersecting corridor.

"Poor, Sovan," his companion, the other guard said softly.

"Who could have done this?" Abu asked angry.

"Someone certainly did it. Perhaps it was some personal enemy? One of our own people with some vendetta? Yet I fear more likely, the Zorrs have been through here. There seem to be too many secret passages for them to have hidden here while we searched the place. We could have missed them. I never sent men deep into the abandoned tunnels below this structure. I did not know they even existed until now."

"Who could have known, Tan?" Abu told me.

"I should have known. I should have counted on the evil cunning of Koth."

As we looked down upon the sad remains of Sovan we heard distant sounds

"...DRAWN SWORDS OUT AND READY..."

of battle coming from behind us. What was this now?

Quickly the three of us ran as fast as we could back into the Great Hall. Here we saw hundreds of Koth's black-robed and masked men barring our exit, and now they charged into the Great Hall.

"Where did *they* come from?" Abu shouted amazed. "I posted half a dozen guards at that entrance. Good men. I saw them there when we left."

"Yes," I told him angry now, "but it was dark and the Zorrs could have infiltrated these rooms. This place must be honeycombed with secret rooms and passageways. There may have been Koth's men dressed as Asudra warriors. Obviously since Sovan is dead they were ready for us and secretly hidden in the lower passages. Who can tell how deep and wide these tunnels and passages go. Or where they go to. Now hundreds of our enemies have escaped right under our noses! Perhaps even Koth himself?"

Both Abu and I felt like fools as we joined our badly outnumbered troops and the Zel clan. No matter how hard I looked at the fleeing Zorrs I did not see Dallia, or even Koth.

Little did I know at the time, for I was told this later, that if I would have looked into the next corridor I would have been rewarded. For there, Koth, and a dozen of his most trusted men, along with their captive Dallia, were making their escape. This I did not know at the time, for there were hundreds of Koth's warriors blocking my way with their swords and attacking us at that very moment.

Meanwhile Koth was making his escape. Where he was going, I could not guess.

CHAPTER 19

We were trapped, yet we all fought fiercely. I had about a hundred good stalwart men with me, along with the eighty-two Zels who had all armed themselves with the weapons of the dead warriors from the Great Hall. So I had a considerable force, but still easily outnumbered by Koth's Zorr fiends. They had us outnumbered by two to one. Nevertheless, the battle went on and was brutal. How long that fight went on I could not say but after a long while it was evident we were winning.

It had been a zig-zag fight from the onset. At first Koth's men had surprised us and had thrown us back, then we rallied, and made a forceful attack upon them that had them pulling back in fear. This conflict had gone back and forth, but gradually the Zorrs were getting the worst of it. I put it to Abu Zel and his Zel clan members, who were enraged at their treatment and were seeking revenge, so they fought like demons giving no quarter. Revenge can be sweet and spur victims onto great courage and victory.

In time the Zorrs were routed, most were killed, and the rest were taken prisoners. Their captain, a man called Croth just laughed when I demanded he tell me where Koth and his group had gone to. Croth seemed to be toying with telling me anything, stalling for time. Then suddenly from nowhere he withdrew a slim dagger and he thrust it into his heart. He screamed and shuddered and then lay motionless. Soon he lay dead his face twisted in a grim deadly laugh. That dagger thrust had silenced Croth forever. It had also silenced any knowledge where Koth had escaped to, along with Dallia's whereabouts.

Koth's power and promises appealed to many men, enslaving minds as well as their wills. His promise of lust, wealth and power appealed to too many. His men's allegiance bordered upon some form of fanaticism as witnessed by the suicide of Captain Croth. Even though Koth's promises of power and riches spoke to many, his power was now crushed. Or so I hoped. Nevertheless, he was still a dangerous foe while at large. I had to track him down and bring to him the justice he deserved.

And he still held Dallia as his captive.

Only a dozen of his men remained alive as prisoners. None of them would talk, though I doubted that Koth had told any of these lower-level minions his plans in any case. What to do next? The thought was weighing heavily upon my mind.

After the conquest of the stronghold and the freedom of the Zels, we all got together and left to go back to Cathor. There had only been about a dozen *zibas* still in the stables, so my force had to walk a long way. I let the women and the few children with us ride upon the huge beasts, and while we did have enough water, we were low on food. If it came to hunger, I knew we might have to slaughter one of the zibas for their meat. If it came to that. Since many of the Zel survivors were women and older men we had to take our time in returning to Cathor, so that it was a full five *talas* from the time the Zorrs attacked us until we reached Cathor.

By the time we reached Cathor the city was no longer under siege. Cathor had surrendered and the people came out to greet Azare and his army as liberators. When I found Hotath and Droth, I asked them what happened, after they had a heartfelt reunion with their father Abu, and all the surviving members of the Zel clan.

"Cathor fell a day after you left, Tan," Hotath told me with a wide grin. "My brother and I were appointed by Azare, Beeg and Ven Og as temporary rulers until our father's return. Once again, the Zel clan will rule in Cathor."

I was happy for the Zels and for the people of Cathor. They had come out of a dark struggle and finally won. Koth's power had apparently been broken in this city, as it had been broken in many others. But was that power destroyed all over Rigel? Koth had escaped after all. Where had he gone? And what of my beloved Dallia? Where might she be? I was constantly thinking of her now, so that as Hotath spoke to me I hardly noticed Droth enter through the side entrance of the room. Nor did I notice who was with him.

"My friend," Droth called out to me as he walked up behind me and got my attention. "You have a visitor."

I instantly turned and looked into the loving eyes of Dallia. My heart leapt with absolute joy. She was alive and unharmed, and here with me now! She was as radiant and lovely as ever.

Droth just smiled, said, "Here is someone who would like to see you again, who you may not know."

I looked from Dallia to Droth, "What do you mean?"

"Prince Tan Alvaka," Droth spoke up with a shy grin, "I would like to introduce you to the Lady Dallia Zel."

It took me a moment before I realized the meaning of those words, of what Droth had said.

"It is true, Tan, my love," Dallia's lovely voice told me as we held each other in our arms. "I have been speaking to Hotath and Droth, who I have discovered are my long-lost brothers. Long lost, but still of the same Zel clan blood. Remember I told you I never knew my father, yet my mother was the Princess Alea. I have found out while speaking with these warriors—my brothers—that they never knew their mother also, but that it is said by many that I look very much like her."

I was astounded, shocked, but utterly joyful.

Dallia continued. "It did not take long for me to find out that Alea was their own mother as she was mine. Nor that Abu is my true father. I have never been so happy, my love, for now I know I have a true family—and a true lover! And my evil stepfather Koth is gone from my life. This is the real family that I have lost and not known existed for so long until this moment. I am so happy."

Dallia and I held each other for the longest time until Abu in good humor separated us, while all there laughed happily. "Enough now, until the wedding."

I smiled, feeling a bit embarrassed. I looked at the young woman in my arms taking a deep breath to assure myself that after so long a time we were truly together. That this all was real.

"How did you get here?" I asked Dallia.

Dallia gave a slim smile. It was then that she and Droth told me the story of what happened. It seemed that as soon as Cathor had fallen, Droth went north with a small group of warriors. It was there that they ran into Koth encamped with a dozen of his warrior bodyguards, with Dallia as his hostage. Koth, unlike any of us, had always known the truth that Dallia was Abu Zel's daughter and Droth's sister. That was why he valued her so highly. Droth and his men had no choice but to lay down their arms as Koth, holding a knife to Dallia's throat, rode away with his men to escape across the plains.

Droth added, "It seems that Koth was met in Cathor by warriors from Bamhor who were under orders to aid Koth as long as he brought Dallia to their emperor Selek. But as Koth fled with his Bamhor allies they were overtaken again by me and my men. The men of Bamhor while holding Dallia captive were forced to give battle and were engaged heavily by my men. As the battle raged, they, nor I, noticed Koth and his men slip away and escape over a small hill.

At the end of the battle, Dallia was safe, the warriors from Bamhor were retreating and Koth and his men were gone. He has never been seen since. It seemed the only problem now was Koth's disappearance, and it plagued me most heavily.

I heard this story and vowed that Koth would not escape me!

"No city, no individual will be safe on Rigel until this mad man is captured or killed." I said firmly, a promise that I saw as destiny.

However, for now, the best thing was that Dallia was safe and that she and I were once again together. Now no one could keep us apart. Koth's secret outlaw cult of Zorr was smashed, no longer a threat, and while he had escaped, we all felt that his capture was just a matter of time and that he could do us no real harm any longer.

I did not know how wrong I was!

CHAPTER 20

Much time had passed since the disappearance of Koth. The four seasons of Rigel had come and passed twice but the man who was the leader of the secret cult of Zorr had disappeared and was never heard from again. I knew that he was not dead, but in hiding, no doubt working on some new nefarious scheme of conquest. The arrogance of the man had been incredible! He had come so close to having his secret cult of

Zorr conqueror all the free cities of Rigel. Now the fearsome black-robed and face masked warriors of his outlaw empire were no more. Koth was just a bad memory these days, though a very vivid and fearful one that none of us could ever forget. I feared that we had not heard the last of him and that at some point in the future we would hear from him once again.

Dallia and I in the meantime had been married and had a child on the way. We now lived in Asudra, the beloved city of my birth, and Dallia and I were very happy there as we awaited the birth of our baby.

Meanwhile, warriors from all the free cities of Rigel were on the lookout for the notorious outlaw Koth. A massive reward had been posted for his arrest, or death. All the inhabitants of the southern cities, those south of the Hills of Mystery were constantly on the lookout for him.

Then I heard a report from one of my agents in Vorba that Koth had recently been seen there. I jumped at the possibility of finally catching him and bringing him to justice, and made ready to leave immediately to catch him, though Dallia tried to restrain me.

"He is deadly and dangerous, very cunning," Dallia spoke up in dire concern, which I was aware of, and that she knew of only too well.

"I know that," I told her as I kissed her tenderly and rubbed the swollen roundness of her belly, and the baby that was growing within, "but I must go, my love. You know that."

"Yes, but be careful, Tan," she cried sadly. "He is a vile monster, and slippery as a dirty *kuloth*, the most poisonous and dangerous of all slithering reptiles."

"I will," I told her. "But he shall not escape me this time."

I meant that, for I knew that with Koth still alive and loose, Dallia and I would never truly be safe—and we had a baby to consider as well now. There was no alternative but for me to get Koth—capture him—or kill him!

Then I rode on to my destiny—my thoughts awhirl to capture or kill Koth - or to go down to my own doom. I planned to enter Vorba incognito under the guise of a trader in fine cloth who was looking to buy goods to sell in my native city of Asudra. Vorba was well known for its quality cloth and finery.

Once in Vorba I entered a tavern to get something to eat and learn the layout of things there. I asked many questions but trying to do so without causing any undo suspicion or attention to myself. I looked around and was surprised to see an old friend. His name was Sontar. I went over and joined him at his table, and he welcomed me with good hallow comradeship.

We had been sitting and drinking and talking for a long time of old days and old battles. Catching up on what had befallen us since so many seasons past.

"Come on you two!" the fat tavern keeper eventually growled at us impatiently. The tavern had all but emptied out by then, but we had hardly noticed. "What is this? It is late! It is dark out; you both have to go now!"

Sontar and I just laughed good naturedly. We had been sitting and talking about old times for so long, that with his latest story finished, we realized the tavern keeper was right. We saw how late the time truly was.

I paid the tavern keeper his money for the meal and gave him a little something extra. This unexpected boon brought a large smile to his fat face.

"Now I need a place to sleep," I told the man. "Do you know such a place?"

The tavern keeper gave me a wry grin. "Sir, surely, I have a fine room. If I may have your name and another piece of your silver, I will gladly give a gentleman such as yourself a most lovely room that I have upstairs."

"This is Prince Tan Al..." Sontar informed the tavern keeper, before I was able to put my hand out to stay his words.

Quickly I let onto Sontar that I wished to remain anonymous. I did not want anyone to know my true identity. The tavern keeper's eyes grew wide at Sontar's slip of speech and then seemed to suddenly shrug as if he had become disinterested. Why he did this, I could not tell. I wondered about what it might mean.

"I am Tanvak... a trader in fine cloth from Asudra," I told the tavern man as I handed him another silver coin. "I need a room to sleep for the night."

He gladly took the coin and then showed me to a room upstairs. He probably realized he could have charged me more for the room than he had first told me. He was obviously annoyed now with himself that he had not done so. Sontar came with me and when we were sure we were alone Sontar spoke.

"I am sorry, Tan—or Tanvak as you apparently wish to be called now," he said curiously, "but tell me, why all the secrecy? Why do you come to our troubled city?"

Indeed, Vorba was now a troubled city, for Ven Og the emperor, had two seasons ago somehow much changed from a beloved monarch, to a most hated tyrant. I had heard stories of this, dark tales of murder and atrocities committed under Van Og's orders, but I would not believe them. The emperor I knew was a middle-aged man, a brave warrior and good friend, a true comrade. A little over four seasons ago he had taken control of Vorba from Koth's men. Like his father, he had begun his reign as a beloved leader, but now things had definitely changed here. He had changed. I wondered why? How?

"Why are you here, Tan?" Sontar asked me curiously, looking at me carefully. "Not because of Ven Og?"

"No," I admitted with a thoughtful look. "You remember me speaking to you about that man, the outlaw, Koth?"

"Of course," he replied, a light coming into his eyes.

"Well," I added, "Koth was reportedly seen in Vorba recently and I am here to find him."

Sontar nodded thoughtfully.

How I was going to find Koth, I had no idea. The only clue I had was that an Asudra warrior now mysteriously dead had told a tale that their emperor, and the outlaw Koth, were in a conspiracy with someone named Lord Ombro. This Lord Ombro was one of the wealthiest of Vorba merchants and a power in the city. Then the warrior, under another of Ven Og's ghastly orders, had been killed.

"Lord Ombro you say? He is very powerful indeed," Sontar told me as he gave me a look communicating caution. "He was thought to be totally loyal, but there have been rumors. I do not know any more. I wish you luck. If Lord Ombro and this outlaw Koth have joined forces, you are in for a difficult task indeed."

I nodded gravely, for I knew he was correct.

I saw Sontar out of my room into the hallway. I let him know I must remain at the tavern, and that I could not take a room at his family home, so as not to cause suspicion. I told him I would seek an audience with this Lord Ombro the next day. After Sontar left, I sat down and did much thinking before I went to much needed sleep.

However, even in slumber, dark thoughts churned in my mind as I tried to find comforting sleep from a long time of travel. How could I capture Koth, if indeed the man in question was Koth?

Sontar had his own troubles also, and I was concerned for him, for he was from a wealthy family which Ven Og now sought to destroy. Revolt, Sontar had told me, was beginning to surface in secret places and in defiant whispers in Vorba. At that time little had Sontar and I realized our two separate problems might be connected. In time I finally found slumber and had been asleep for a short while when I heard footsteps in the corridor outside my room. What is this, I thought?

They were heavy footsteps from a large man—or men—perhaps a warrior? I was not sure if I should pay attention to this or not, but I knew to be ever on my guard. My sword and dagger were close by. It may have just been a late-night fellow returning to his room drunk and noisy. Or...?

Then I heard a familiar voice whispering, "Silence now, and remember, the master wants this man alive."

It was the voice of the tavern keeper without any doubt, muffled but it was surely him, but what could he be about? I steeled myself alert and ready for treachery. I knew I was soon to find out just what this was all about if they entered my room.

Then they entered my room.

CHAPTER 21

T he door to my room opened very slowly and very quietly. It was alarming. I made a grab for my sword, holding the hilt tightly as I watched intently the two images entering my room. I saw out of the corner of my eye that the tavern keeper was there with four men. All of them I noticed were formerly of Koth's personal bodyguard. I lay upon the bed, faking sleep but watching them intently and ready to strike out, my hand upon the pommel of my sword under the blanket—but something stopped me.

The four crept upon me carefully. I saw no weapons in their hands other than clubs, and the tavern keeper stood behind them, urging them forward in harsh whispers.

"Remember, do not kill him!" the tavern keeper ordered his four minions in a low voice. "Take him captive. The master wants him alive."

I remained motionless still feigning sleep. I knew I could rise up in a fury and fight the four, defeat them, then force the information I needed about Koth from them, but then I saw a better way. Maybe not so wise, but it would surely work. At least I hoped so and it seemed the most direct route to get to what I wanted—and that was Koth. I knew these men would not be aware of much information about Koth if I defeated them and questioned them. So I decided to try a different plan. I decided to allow them to capture me. This seemed to be the most direct way to get me to Koth, even though I would have to chance a few hard blows. No problem for any true warrior of Rigel. I had finally, after so long a time, made contact with agents of Koth. I would let them take me captive and then I would be brought to him. Then I would capture him. Or kill him. I preferred the latter. I knew I was taking a big chance, but the fact that these men wanted to take me alive offered me a possibility of getting to Koth. So I allowed it to happen. Soon I was struck upon the head and while in some pain, I pretended to slip into unconsciousness.

I faked unconsciousness and was roughly placed into a sack of some kind. Then I was carried around for what seemed like many *tals*. Later I was taken out of the sack and found myself placed upon a large couch. I looked around me and found that I was in a rather magnificent chamber—not my tawdry tavern room at all. As I sat up to clear my senses, I saw the four men who had captured me standing nearby. Waiting. Waiting for some order. They were now dressed in the regular fighting harness and uniform of warriors from Vorba. A large heavily armored and well-dressed man suddenly entered the chamber. He looked at me curiously and took a seat in one of the lavish couches across from me.

"I am Lord Ombro," he announced simply, allowing a sly smile. "I heard that you were seeking me out for a meeting? It has been a long time, has it not, Tan Alvaka?"

Slowly I recognized Lord Ombro by his voice. *I knew this man!* He was a man I had known many seasons ago. He had been the commander of the Zorr stronghold in the Hills of Mystery. He was the sadistic fiend who had imprisoned Droth Zel and myself in the Pit of the Dead. The man had gone missing after the fall of the Zorr stronghold. Now I knew where he had gone to. He was Lord Ombro of Vorba!

I looked at him in anger recalling all his cruel treatment of me and my companion.

"Yes, I see that you are surprised. Well, I am also a wealthy and respectable merchant here," he told me with boastful arrogance. "and I am a good friend, you might say, to Ven Og emperor of Vorba."

If I was not bound helpless I would have jumped upon him and strangled the life out of him. As it was, all I could do was spit in defiance.

Lord Ombro laughed heartily, "You are such a fool. You persist in trying to find my master, but you never shall do so. Instead he has found you! Now it is for him to decide upon your fate."

"He will pay, and so will you!" I shouted at my captor in anger.

"Defiant to the end, eh, Tan Alvaka? Well, that end shall come very soon, I promise you."

Lord Ombro laughed victoriously at his own wit, then ordered me to be taken from his presence. I was marched out of the room through the building and placed in a dark dank cell that I assumed was deep beneath his palace. As the door to my prison shut the guard spoke to me in a mocking voice, "Tomorrow, when he is here, you shall see the Master Zorr, himself."

"Good!" I spoke up defiant.

As I lay in my small cell, I realized I had to somehow stop Koth before he began his mad scheme of conquest all over again. It was obvious he had considerable resources and followers I had never known about. He was not done and dead as many of us had thought. I just wondered what his game was now. Revenge and more conquest, no doubt.

The night passed without incident and the next morning I awoke to hear the passing of footsteps in the corridor outside my cell. At first I thought it was the guards coming to escort me to Lord Ombro's presence, but I soon learned it was but a single warrior carrying food.

I feigned sleep so that no sooner had he opened the door to my cell that I flew upon him, knocking the sword from his hand, and hurling him to the ground. It was a quick matter of work to knock him out, and then tie him with his own clothing. Picking up his sword, I raced out of the cell and into the corridor, now free to seek out Koth.

I assumed that Koth had returned to Vorba and was staying in Lord Ombro's palace. So he had to be somewhere in this building, or so I hoped. I ran up to the main floor, carefully going to room after room, checking them thoroughly, always keeping to the shadows so as not to be seen until I came to the very chamber that I had been with Lord Ombro one *tala* previous. Here I carefully looked inside to see who might be there. What I saw was the haughty Lord Ombro and Ven Og emperor of Vorba in deep conversation.

Ven Og's voice, after a few moments changed drastically to a familiar sound. Then from my place of concealment, I was astounded to see Ven Og pull at a patch of his dark hair that pulled off the image of his face! Instantly I realized the truth! Now I knew why the emperor of Vorba had changed his personality so drastically, so much so that even loyal Sontar now opposed him. I could well believe all the horrid tales of Ven Og's recent rule, for the man I saw before me was not Ven Og at all—on the contrary—it was the hated outlaw Koth! The most wanted supreme criminal of my world!

I looked on in shock and a growing dark fear. How had this happened? Koth had not only escaped, he had somehow found a way to completely impersonate the emperor of this noble city. He looked and spoke exactly like the true emperor of Vorba, who might for all I knew already be dead, murdered like his father before him, who Koth had killed over six seasons ago.

As I watched in fascination at this meeting, an insane hatred urged me to charge right into that chamber and kill Koth on the spot. But I held back, curious as to what these two fiends were planning so studiously. It was crucial that I learn what they were up to. So I waited, patient and listened to their words.

It was Lord Ombro who continued speaking. "My Lord, Koth," he said in a most conciliatory tone, "that upstart pest Tan Alvaka is back and causing us trouble. He is now in a cell below my palace and will be put to death at your pleasure."

"You have done well," Koth told his minion, then he snorted, "Very well, indeed. I want Tan Alvaka dead right after I leave, and I want his head sent to the Vorban Palace where I shall add it to my collection."

"Very well, Master," Ombro told him with a sick smile that was joined in by Koth.

Koth then grew serious with a savage grin, "I have come because I have news. I have just struck up an alliance with Kromo of the city of Podool. He will offer powerful assistance in my plan, and even now is working on a new secret weapon that will bring all of the cities on Rigel to their knees. No one shall be able to stop me this time."

Just at that moment a pair of warriors who had turned down the corridor saw me listening outside the door of Ombro's chamber. They recognized me as the escaped prisoner and with shouts and yells, soon had the entire palace alert to my presence.

I quickly drew my sword as these guards came at me and soon found myself fighting furiously in another battle for my life. I was soon backed into a corner, and before me now stood a dozen of Lord Ombro's swordsmen. However, they could not all come at me at once. Lord Ombro himself had long since locked the door so that my avenue of retreat into his chamber was blocked.

Shortly thereafter I saw Lord Ombro at the other end of the corridor calling for his men to cut me down. None of them could do so, of course. Not yet.

"Come at me! Come on!" I dared them, as my blade cut them down quickly, forcing them to move back in fear. Though I was outnumbered, I was the far better swordsman. They could not follow the swiftness of my blade as it cut a bloody swath of ghastly wounds through them. One after another of them moved to get away from my frantic blade. I could see their fear of me now. And it was growing!

I was cutting my foes down at a steady pace but they kept coming at me and I was tiring. After a time I only faced two most reluctant warriors, both too fearful to offer me much resistance. Lord Ombro was behind them urging them onward against me with wild threats and promises. I smiled grimly as I pressed his two men back to fall upon him. Meanwhile, Koth was nowhere to be seen.

Now there were only the four of us in that long corridor. I pressed Ombro's men still farther back, and then quickly dropped both of them with two quick slashes. Now it was just Ombro and myself, face to face. He gritted his teeth, looked to see that there was nowhere to run, and quickly drew his sword as he backed away from me slowly. There was terror written large upon his face.

"Surrender and you shall be spared," I told him.

In answer he came at me in a wild charge, trying to pummel my head relentlessly. His attack was as if done by a child and it was easy for me to dodge.

Lord Ombro had at one time been a loyal leader of Vorba and a trusted friend of the Zel clan. Now he had sold them out to join in Koth's twisted plans for world conquest. He had also been the author of much suffering by the Zels and myself. I had a debt to be paid to him.

I moved towards Lord Ombro hard now, with vengeance in my eyes. I was no longer wasting any time with him. He would not surrender. Then so be it! In no time I knocked his sword with a hard clash and it flew from his grasp. He was shocked and uttered a cry of fear. Then my blade was at his unprotected throat. He begged me for mercy. The great Lord Ombro had turned into a terror-stricken lump of quivering jelly. I could not help but be disgusted by his cowardice. I cut lightly at his throat, the few drops of blood dripping down his neck.

"That is just a sample of what is to come if you do not speak up now and tell me what I want to know," I growled at him.

He shivered, "What? What? Spare me! Anything!"

"What has Koth done with Ven Og? Where is he?"

Ombro would not speak, only scream and cry in whimpering terror.

"Tell me! Where has Koth gone?" I demanded impatiently.

He did not reply, only continued to whimper like the vast coward he was.

"Tell me now!" I shouted into his face, shaking him mightily.

"Have mercy," he pleaded with me.

I growled, "You want mercy now, but you gave no mercy!"

"I never meant to harm you," he lied in a gasping lisp.

"No? You enjoyed it!" I told him angrily.

I had planned to take him captive. Then from out of nowhere the sly fiend pulled out a slim dagger and tried to plunge it into my heart. I knocked his dagger to the floor.

So I just slid my blade deeper into the man's neck, just near the artery. The blood was now flowing more thickly down his throat, and he screamed out in abject terror.

"What has Koth done with Ven Og?" I repeated, losing my patience.

He whimpered and then quieted down. He was bleeding out. He was slowly dying.

"The next cut will be more severe and it will spurt out your life's blood in a gushing stream. You do not want me to do that," I asked him forcefully.

"Ven Og is kept as a prisoner in Kromo's palace in Podool," he replied the terror in his face growing. "Please let me go."

"Where has Koth gone to?" I barked.

"He has fled to the palace. Warriors are on the way here now, let me go, and

I shall help you to escape this building."

I knew Lord Ombro was no threat to me. He was only a small link in Koth's deadly chain. It was Koth who I was really after. So I acceded to Ombro's wish and allowed him to lead me out of his chamber. We quickly walked down many corridors until I came to the outside gardens at the back of the palace grounds. Here I could climb over the wall and escape to find Sontar.

When I was atop the wall, ready to spring to the other side, I could see a host of Vorba guards advancing from Lord Ombro's palace.

"Kill him!" I heard Lord Ombro shout to his men. "Don't let him get away!"

Lord Ombro seemed to have regained his courage now that so many armed guards had come to his aid. He ran towards me, and before I was over the wall, he grabbed at me, trying to pull me down. Then from somewhere in his tunic he pulled out another deadly dagger, to hold me off as his guards drew closer to me. Their swords were out and ready to taste my blood. I would let them come and taste the sharpness of my blade.

Well they came on, but two can play at that game. I had lost my patience with the man. At that point I thrust my sword out and deep into Lord Ombro's traitorous heart. He died instantly. Then I quickly jumped over the palace wall and ran onto the dark city street beyond.

I ran a few blocks where I hid in an alley while the Vorba guardsmen searched the area for me without success. Then when they passed me by, I left and made my way cautiously and under cover in the shadows to the house of Sontar.

Everything went well and soon I was at the door to Sontar's well-appointed family home. In no time I was seated in a small private chamber with my friend, Sontar. I told him what had befallen me since he had left my room in the tavern one *tala* ago.

"I feared that tavern man was not trustworthy," Sontar told me with a wry grin.

I nodded, "And he certainly proved it."

"It is all too strange to believe, but it explains Ven Og's brutal behavior lately," he said with alarm in his eyes.

"We must get to the palace and dispose of Koth," I told him quickly, stressing the urgent need for action. "Then I need to go to Podool and free Ven Og. He is imprisoned in the palace of Kromo, who is some other highly placed secret ally of Koth."

"I will come with you too, Tan," he said.

"Good, I shall surely need all the help I can get."

"It would be better if we do this mission alone, just the two of us" Sontar told me carefully, "for it will be easier for two sly men to enter the palace in secret, than an army."

"Most of the palace guards are in Koth's employ. Would it be possible to arouse the people here to storm the palace?"

Sontar smiled a glowing grin. Then he told me to await his return, as he quickly left the room.

When Sontar came back he brought with him a dozen men of his clan along with others, who were of different clans and families. All of them had their hate of Koth in common.

Sontar and I explained to the men about Koth's impersonation of their good emperor Ven Og. It was a hard thing for most of them to believe. All however wanted the tyrant out of power—whoever he might be.

Sontar and I gave each man explicit instructions to gather as many followers as possible and come to the palace at midnight. Then, exactly on the twelfth *tal*, at midnight, they were to storm the palace and kill or take prisoner as many of the palace guards as possible.

I noticed that many of the friends of Sontar, like Sontar himself, wore the Vorba military uniform. I only hoped we would win this battle—which quickly might turn into an all-out civil war. Then with the plan discussed fully and understood by all, Sontar and I left for the palace to capture, or kill, Koth.

It was perhaps four *tals* towards midnight when we reached the Vorba palace where we knew Koth would be surrounded by his personal bodyguard.

As we entered the palace grounds we were met by only minimal opposition. We made quick work of these few guardsmen. I wondered why the security was apparently so lax, but Sontar said he was sure that once inside the palace we would find a veritable army to resist us. I hoped this would not prove to be true, but my men and I were ready.

As we entered the place each of us hoped that he would be the man who would finally thrust a sword blade into Koth's putrid heart.

CHAPTER 22

The palace of the emperor of Vorba was an impressive building, yet not as awe-inspiring as the Florian Palace in Cathor, or the Asurdan Palace of my home city. The Vorba structure was beautiful, yet relatively plain, but of more concern to us as we entered was not the architectural qualities, but that it was so heavily guarded. It also appeared to be a citadel, rather than a palace.

As Sontar and I stood outside on the grounds wondering how we were going to break down the massive front gate and then the heavy doors of the place, I saw a wagon that was being pulled by a massive *osk*. The huge wagon was being pulled by rather unruly beast guided by an old man who brought it to the palace.

As the old man approached, I saw him talk heatedly with the four men on guard at the palace gate. By then Sontar and I made our way quietly along the shadows of the wall of the palace to the side of the wagon. Then when no one was looking we jumped into the back of the wagon and quickly buried ourselves under the silk and hide coverings.

We found the wagon filled with many choice fruits and vegetables, doubtless for the kitchens of the emperor's palace. We began burrowing down under the boxes and sacks of fruits so that we were completely hidden, and it was a good thing we did. After a few more *bans*, more moments of arguing, the guards came over to the wagon and uncovered the furs to look at all the fruits and vegetables beneath.

The guards looked over everything most carefully, poking and prodding. What they found was a wagon full of fruits and vegetables, just as it appeared to be, but for some reason this did not stop them in their search. This had me a bit worried, for it appeared they knew something more than we thought they should. Had they seen something? Had someone talked? Or betrayed us? Soon we heard their officer give an ominous order.

"Pierce the contents of the wagon with your sword blades," he ordered his men, and they drew their long sharp-bladed weapons. "Make sure this old man is carrying only fruits and vegetables as he says."

I looked at Sontar startled, and he looked at me nervously, but there was nothing we could do. We must be silent, even if cut by one of the guard's blades. We must keep silent. From the floor of the wagon, I could see the old

IT ALSO APPEARED TO BE A CITADEL...

man look askance at the guard commander's order. He was angry now.

"No! This is outrageous! You are going to ruin my goods—and the emperor's food!" the old man argued, shouting for the guards to stop their foolishness and for them to allow him to pass into the palace unmolested. "You know me! I come here time after time. You are destroying my best crop. Now I will not be paid!"

For that the old man was smacked across the face while the guardsmen continued to thrust their swords into the wagon full of fruit and vegetables.

Sontar and I lay motionless and quiet. I do not think either of us breathed, but of course we did—but most carefully. We saw the blades as they were thrust among us, some very close, some even cutting us slightly. We remained silent. I realized I had been hit in the arm twice, but they were not serious wounds. Sontar had been stabbed once along the leg, yet neither of us made any noise or movement. To do so meant instant death.

Sontar looked at me and whispered lightly, "What if they notice our blood on their swords…?"

I nodded. "Then we are surely doomed."

However, the guards soon grew annoyed at what they considered to be a useless pursuit, and soon stopped their efforts and Sontar and I felt the wagon move forward. We were being allowed to pass into the area behind the palace, by the kitchen.

Within a few *bans* the wagon stopped again, and the old man left. I assume he went into the palace kitchen. Seeing our chance now we both raised ourselves up and took a look at our surroundings. We were in the grounds at the rear of the palace, and while the wall was now guarded, the rear palace entrance was not.

Quickly Sontar and I jumped out of the wagon without being detected by the guards ringed in a line upon the palace wall. Immediately we rolled into the bushes at the side of the huge building and carefully made our way along the building edge to the rear entrance. Neither of us were badly wounded from the guard's swords and our sword arms had not been injured, so it was with renewed confidence that we entered the palace through the kitchen. Suddenly we heard footsteps and hid behind a large curtain as perhaps fifty warriors ran past us. When they were gone, Sontar looked at me and spoke softly, "That was close. Now where do we go?"

"We go after Koth. He is playing at being emperor. Do you know the way to the emperor's personal suite?"

Sontar nodded and led the way, and soon we were on our way. We went most carefully and made sure we were not seen. We saw no one on the way, and as we neared a corner in the corridor on the upper level, Sontar assured me that the emperor's apartments were just around the next corner.

As we reached the next corridor we stopped suddenly. Down the end of the corridor there were at least a hundred guards. There were many rooms that opened into this main corridor with many men walking about. This was doubtless the headquarters of Koth's bodyguard. I feared we had blundered into something that could end our mission very soon, in a very bad way.

Two men looked at us and one ordered, "You two, come here!"

"Who, us?" I asked simply.

"Yes, you two," the guard continued impatiently. "Move when I call you!"

"Sorry, we have been called away by the commander," I told him, making up what I hoped was a plausible story, then we turned and went around the corner out of his sight.

"What…!" I heard the man shout, then bark an order.

Soon two men came down the corridor towards us. As they neared us, Sontar and I moved back around the corner. They came around the corner and we were ready for them. No sooner did their body make the turn of the corner—so that they were now not visible to their fellows—then Sontar and I took them down. It was quick and by surprise. They never knew what hit them.

Sontar and I quickly stripped the two guards and put on their uniforms, now we were part of the bodyguard of the emperor of Vorba. We bound and gagged the two actual Vorba guards and put them into a nearby empty room back down the hall. They would be unconscious for quite a while since I had given them each a good hard knock to the head.

Now, Sontar and I, dressed and acting as if we were Koth's loyal Vorba bodyguards, walked boldly down the enemy laden corridor. To the enemy we were only two more of their comrades and we smiled and nodded to them most pleasantly as we passed them by. No one questioned us as we walked towards the guarded chambers of Koth, the impersonator of the city's emperor.

"Halt!" the guardsman outside Koth's door demanded of us. He looked directly at Sontar. "On what business do you want to see Emperor Ven Og?"

"We bear urgent news to bring before the eyes of Ven Og only. There is a plot of a revolt against our beloved emperor," Sontar stated firmly, to my surprise. I thought he was giving away our plans of revolution, but instantly I realized that it did not take a genius to know that the city was a powder keg ready to explode at any moment. So his ruse was surely a plausible one.

The Guard nodded but stood silent, he did not seem to know what to do until an officer came over to us.

"What is going on here?" the officer asked, curious.

The guard explained, and the officer looked at us carefully.

We said nothing yet. I took a deep breath.

"That is good news. Good job fellows!" the officer told us with a grim smile. "Now we will nip this revolt before it even begins. But you will have to wait, Ven Og is in an important conference with Kromo of Podool."

Sontar and I nodded in understanding, as our eyes burned at this news, a grim smile crossed our faces. For now we knew that Koth was in that chamber—and with him was the emperor of Podool! This might make a good catch, if we could pull it off.

At that moment Sontar and I looked at each other and just smiled as we instantly drew our swords and quickly cut down the guard and his officer. Then we entered the emperor's luxurious apartments, dragging the two dead bodyguards inside with us. We placed their bodies in a corner behind some furniture. Quickly I turned the door lock for I knew that soon the rest of the bodyguards would be banging heavily upon the massive door. We were in the emperor's private apartments and the enemy was outside banging upon the door to get in at us.

I took a deep breath and looked nervously at Sontar. "That door should hold them for more than a few *ban*."

He just looked at me and smiled, indicating I should look behind me.

I turned around and there I faced my greatest nemesis, Koth of Cathor, the leader of the secret Zorr criminal cult. He did not appear as I had imagined. The scenario was incredible to me and shocking.

For the sight that Sontar and I saw shocked us completely. The chamber lay empty, except for Koth's bloody body.

"Is it him?" Sontar asked me in shock.

"Yes, certainly, I am sure," I said, then I looked at him more carefully. "At least I think so."

"Look at him," Sontar asked incredulous.

"Is he dead?" I blurted stunned by the bloody sight, realizing that if he was in fact dead, I felt I had been somehow terribly cheated.

"I think not."

"What happened?" I asked.

"He is not dead, Tan," Sontar stated quickly as he looked closely at the body. We each rushed over to the bloody body, disappointed that we had been cheated from striking the death blow against Koth.

We discovered that Koth was alive, but fatally wounded and mad with pain, but as he saw me, he gave out a faint laugh of absolute derision.

"You have been cheated of killing me," he spoke up with a wild laugh.

"Who did this to you?" I asked angry.

"It... It was that traitorous fat *osk*, Kromo," Koth whispered painfully in wrathful anger at the betrayal. "He even took the woman. Now I shall never have my revenge upon you, Tan Alvaka, for your ruination of all my plans for the conquest of Rigel."

I looked at him in incomprehensible scrutiny.

"What woman!" I demanded, but he did not speak again. I could see he was dying, and at such a painful speed it gave me at least some small measure of justice. I offered to play to his need for revenge, to get some answers. "Tell us all about Kromo, and we will revenge you,"

Koth was going to die soon, and I wanted him to speak of what he knew before then. I wanted to know about this man called Kromo, who was said to be the emperor of Podool. Meanwhile fear welled up in my gut at the mention of this 'woman' who was his captive. Who was she? Was she, in fact, my Dallia? How and why would this Kromo want to get revenge against me through any woman? This much I demanded from Koth.

He merely laughed bitterly. "Do you not remember when Asudra sacked Podool?"

"Of course, but why…" I answered, then remembered. "I was the leader of the charge that took down the city."

"Yes, so you see," Koth weakly replied, "this Kromo is a great scientist from Podool who has always hated the destroyers of his city. Together we planned a way to conqueror Asudra and then we would conquer all of Rigel. The traitor…."

"What of the woman?" I demanded fearfully.

With renewed strength Koth looked at me and just laughed, enjoying my discomfiture. "As you suspect, she is the Lady Dallia, kidnapped the day before and now on her way to Podool. There she shall die after Kromo satisfies himself with her. She was to be my gift to him for our alliance—but he just took her from me. He betrayed me when my forces grew weak. All my grand plans gone, the gutter-spawned creature…"

I shook with rage at learning this news of my poor lady in the hands of our new enemy.

Now coughing blood, the tyrant and outlaw of Rigel breathed his last and suddenly died before me, his life sputtering away in a few gasping breathes. I looked at him with ill-concealed contempt. Koth had left a bloody legacy with his schemes, and maybe even worse now in the form of this monster Kromo of Podool. I had never heard of this man, yet he must have been of some importance in Podool before the destruction of the city. The most important thing for me now was to find Dallia. Somehow, I would have to save her, and then I would kill this Kromo for taking her away. I vowed it to all the gods of Rigel.

As Koth lay dead, and the warriors outside continued to pound their weapons upon the door to his chamber—not knowing of his death—we heard screams and curses from the palace grounds. It was the battle for Vorba. The city seemed to be in revolt all around us.

Soon many of the warriors pounding upon the door went away as thousands of angry citizens broke down the wall, entered the palace grounds and then the palace itself. Fighting raged everywhere. The warriors in the hallway outside our chamber fought, died, or all ran off.

When we were sure the enemy guards had all gone, Sontar and I unlocked the door and found ourselves immediately rushed by four burly guards we had not expected to be there. So not all of Koth's men had retreated. That was fine by me. Sontar and I made quick work of the lead two and then the other two simply ran away to join their cowardly comrades.

Now Sontar left me to take command of the revolutionists while factions of the palace guard vied with each other for leadership since they had discovered that their emperor was dead. A power vacuum needed to be filled.

I went back to Koth's chamber to look upon his dead body for the last time, and found it—gone! Koth's body was gone! Where was it? What had happened to it? I assumed that some fervid supporters had appropriated his corpse for some funeral rite. That seemed to be the logical reason and I did not overly concern myself about that at the time. Nevertheless, I heard a tiny voice within the corner of my mind whispering words I did not want to think about, and so I wondered… Where was he? Could he still be alive? Did he, in fact, have some dark power from the Underworld of Rigel?

In the meantime, Sontar's group was crushing the enemy defenders, the revolution was in good hands. I decided it was time for me to leave Vorba. I was anxious to ride to Podool as quickly as possible to save Dallia from this new enemy.

As I ran across the palace grounds to the stables to take a *ziba* to ride to Podool, I suddenly realized Kromo's identity. I recalled that he was an outlawed scientist and was thought to be dead many years ago. He was a brilliant but mad scientist who was also the head of the Assassins Guild of Podool. A most dangerous man. This is the same group that so long ago had murdered my father. Indeed, I was sure Dallia had much to fear from a fiend like Kromo. Picking the swiftest *ziba* I could find, I mounted the ponderous animal and raced out of the war-torn city of Vorba towards the ruined city of Podool.

CHAPTER 23

I was riding as hard as my ponderous mount could manage, pushing the poor beast to it's swiftest extent. It was a continuous all *tala* ride before I saw the dead city of Podool far in the distance.

My thoughts were constantly on Dallia and her safety as I raced towards the dead city. It had once been a beautiful and thriving center of trade but since the war it was now only a ruined heap. It had lost most of its population, even though many inhabitants had held on and were slowly rebuilding some parts of the city. I looked upon it carefully. It had seen much damage. Mostly it was a great mass of rubble and ruins.

I rode closer and wondered where in this mass of ruin I would find Dallia. It seemed impossible. I had no idea where to begin my search and knew I did not have a lot of time to find her. I felt time was of the essence. I must find her quickly before something dreadful happened. As I entered the city, I was still wearing the fighting harness of a bodyguard of the Vorba emperor, and seeing this I was greeted as an ally and allowed to enter the city by the few guards still on duty. Little did they realize that I had been the author of all this disaster many turns of the seasons long ago.

I tried to figure out what had happened to the city since then. New leaders came to control the populace. A man named Kromo seemed to rule now. Why Kromo had killed Koth I could not imagine, unless he wanted Asudra destroyed—while Koth wanted my city taken intact to add as part of his vision for empire. This later, I found out was the actual reason for their falling out, but it did not matter to me then. Only Dallia mattered!

As I rode my great beast down the rubble-strewn streets I saw many people at work busily rebuilding homes and shops. In a short while I came across an old man who stood in front of a smoke shop which was already rebuilt and seemed well stocked.

I stopped and questioned the oldster.

"Do you know where I can find the man known as Kromo?" I asked carefully. "I bear important news from Vorba for him about a revolt in the city against Ven Og."

"Lord Kromo?" he asked me most curiously. "You wish to speak to Lord Kromo?"

I nodded. "Yes, I do."

Then the old man smiled and motioned me out of the shop and pointed to a large castle perched upon a high hill above the city.

"There is where you shall find Lord Kromo," he told me nervously, "and may the grim god Ibar protect you, if you do."

"Why is that?" I asked the old man.

"You shall see," he replied ominously.

I tried to engage him in further conversation, but he would not speak any more. So I mounted my beast, thanked the old man, and quickly rode away to the castle. As I rode down the street the old man yelled out to me.

"Do not thank me, warrior, for you shall be sorry."

I then left the city through one of the main gates and rode to the top of a large hill that was not too far from the city. Atop the hill was the bleak castle-like fortress belonging to Lord Kromo of Podool.

As I rode to the entrance of the massive edifice, I was approached by four warriors in the harness and uniform of Podool.

I met the men and spoke with their leader telling them I was a messenger from Vorba. They seemed satisfied that I was one of Kormo's messengers or spies returning with news of the revolt in Vorba. I dismounted and was led into the fortress castle.

It was a grim place. It was a large drafty castle fortress, devoid of furniture or any human artifacts. It was indeed a bleak place as I was led down corridor after corridor into the very room in which Dallia and Ven Og were imprisoned. It was a large room, a laboratory of some sorts, and chained to a far wall were both my Lady Dallia and Ven Og.

"Tan, what are you doing here?" Dallia cried out in shock and sudden fear when she saw me.

"I am here to save you!"

"Save me? You have fallen into their trap! You must escape!" Dallia shouted at me, crying in fear for my life. "It is a trap. Kromo is expecting you."

"Then I am here! Where is he?" I asked boldly.

Then a loud voice boomed throughout the room, "Welcome Tan Alvaka," then I heard a man laugh with sinister joy.

I looked all around me but saw no one!

I spoke hastily with Dallia and then tuned to Ven Og.

"Koth is dead, and your city is in good hands now, the people awaiting your return. Sontar has led a rebellion against Koth and his men and has defeated them all," I explained as I used my sword blade to free Dallia and Ven Og from their chains. However, my blade would not work on the hard metal. I needed a key to release the lock on the chain. Now where could that be? Kromo?

"That is good," Ven Og replied, "but you must be careful here, we are in the hands of an enraged madman."

I found that both Dallia and Ven Og were in decent health, and I tried mightily to free them, but it proved an impossible task. I needed the key to their chains to free them and only Kromo had the key. So where was Kromo? Then I heard once again that mocking voice, though he had not shown himself yet. "Tan Alvaka, finally come to my loving home."

Where was he? Where could I find him?

"Show yourself!" I demanded impatiently. "Come out and meet me in battle!"

As I went to the door leading outside the room, I found that it was now locked.

Now the sinister laughter rang out again in a loud mocking cadence.

"Be careful, my love," Dallia warned me, teary eyed. "Kromo possesses a great secret—the secret of invisibility!"

Invisibility? How could that be? Could that be true? I thought on that a moment most carefully. It explained much about the power of Koth and the weird science that Kromo had at his disposal and had obviously allowed Koth to use to gain his power. So Koth, in reality, had been a vassal of this monster, Kromo! Or was it…? I knew not, nor overly cared at that moment.

"Kromo must be in this chamber hidden somewhere as evidenced by his gross laughter," I told her in impatient anger. "Wait until I find him! Invisibility will not protect him! Do you know how he does it? How can he become invisible?" I asked Dallia.

"I do not know his secret, but be careful, he moves quickly. He may be behind you at any moment with a knife poised at your back."

"I have been a captive here a long time, Tan," Ven Og added in an effort to help. "I have seen him do it. He does become invisible. He does it by swallowing a potion of some kind. Some mixture of herbs he has discovered. He drinks it and then he literally disappears from all eyes."

Just then I saw the door to the room open as if by some form of magic, and then the door closed rapidly. I saw nothing, nor no one at the door. However, moments later I heard a ghastly animalistic roar, and instantly recognized the sound as the fighting call of the dread *sarcoth*, a multi-fanged man-eating carnivore of Rigel. They are as big as a baby *ziba* and are many times more ferocious.

"It is a *sarcoth*, and it is invisible, Tan! He can do that to animals too," Dallia warned me. "Be careful!"

"So this is how Kromo would raise his army to fight against Asudra," I thought out loud. I knew this power would be a most potent weapon in the wrong hands. In the hands of Koth it would have been devastating.

Just then another ghastly laugh rang out within the room.

"You are in here with me now," I shouted knowingly. "Kromo! Show yourself!"

"Yes," the man's voice admitted in a loud tone. "I am here. It is I, Lord Kromo of Podool who shall be the instrument of your demise. I shall kill your friend, and then take your woman for myself, while you watch. Then I shall send my invisible army to destroy your accursed city and everyone in it!"

He laughed once again, with a long sick bone-chilling sound. I knew Kromo had to be in this room with me, but it was a very large room. He could be anywhere. Where was he? I still could not see him. His voice echoed and it was not easy to get a location to where he might be standing.

Slowly I moved towards where I thought his voice was coming from. As I moved closer, I heard the *sarcoth*'s mighty roar now very close. I knew then that I had made a terrible mistake. I had thought I had found Kromo. I had not!

Then I felt invisible fangs digging deeply into my left arm. In a flurry of raging pain, I reached for the *sarcoth* with a mighty swipe of my sword. I rushed forward and cut a hundred vicious strokes and deep thrusts, almost always missing, but a couple of times my sword did taste blood. I saw the creature's blood on the tip of my blade, so I knew I had made contact with the invisible beast somehow. However, I was taking cuts from the claws and fangs also as the beast came at me. So far, I had not received any mortal wound, but I was bloody and weak from the creature's furious attacks.

I fought wildly, and I feared vainly for my life. I heard the cries of Dallia and the shouts of support from Ven Og for my battle. Suddenly, quite by luck, I lunged with my blade into a spot I felt was on target and it hit deeply into the *sarcoth*. With a mighty roar of pain, the creature stiffened and instantly it ended it's attack upon me. Then I heard a loud thump as it hit the ground. Within a heartbeat *ban* I myself fell exhausted to the floor after this battle. I was victorious but the battle was not yet done.

For suddenly I heard ringing mad anger and then felt a sharp kick to my gut. It was Kromo come to finish me off. I ached from half a dozen wounds yet somehow, I managed to grab hold of his invisible figure and with my sword cut into him deep and bloody. Somewhere I felt him fall lifeless to the floor. He did not move.

Now that it was all over, I was exhausted, aching from my wounds, and I fell unconscious to the floor.

I awoke in a large chamber to find myself in pain and heavily bandaged. Here I found my Lady Dallia, Ven Og along with Sontar and a large group of Vorba warriors surrounding me.

"The fortress of Kromo, and the city of Podool itself, are now rid of Kromo's men. Lord Kromo is dead," Sontar told me in a victorious tone. "Lord Kromo was found as a bloody mass of flesh. Once he died his body became visible once more."

"He was invisible," I said remembering.

"No longer," Sontar replied. "His formula is lost with him; I fear lost forever."

I nodded, that was good.

"Dallia is well?" I asked with worry, looking over at her.

"I am well, Tan," I heard her lovely voice answer me.

"What of my city of Vorba?" Ven Og added.

"The revolt was successful. Koth is dead and his cult is destroyed. The people have been told of his treachery and welcome you back, My Lord. Whenever you want, you may return to Vorba and resume your imperial duties with the support and love of your people."

"Ibar and the gods be praised!" Ven Og replied rubbing his numb limbs.

That decided, I quickly grabbed up Dallia into my arms.

"I was so fearful for you, Tan," she told me with loving tenderness. "I thought the *sarcoth* would surely kill you."

"It almost did," I said with a grim laugh. "Actually, I had a plan to lure Kromo out into the open where I could get at him. It worked, but it was not easy. The fool was so sure of himself he had only a small dagger upon his person. That did not protect him."

Then I drew Dallia towards me again and we kissed in a firm embrace.

"Easy," she chided me. "You are still an injured man."

"He doesn't appear to be *that* injured," Sontar replied laughing.

Then Sontar ordered his men to make ready to leave the fortress of the dead Lord Kromo.

"Who will rule Podool now that Lord Kromo is no more?" I asked curiously.

It was then that Sontar brought forth the old man who I had spoken with at the city smoke shop.

"This is Kivar Sen," Sontar said by way of introduction, "he shall rule Podool and build it back to it's former greatness."

"My friend," Kivar said to me in a warm tone, "I told you not to come here. I tried to save you much trouble. Eventually we would have killed Kromo ourselves, but his power of invisibility stopped us since it enabled him to control our vision. It was most terrifying. Now I and all my people thank you. We will rebuild our city into a free city once again."

Then Ven Og, emperor of Vorba, and Sontar of Vorba, left us to go back to their own city, while Dallia and I under escort of a company of Vorba warriors left for our home city of Asudra to await the birth of our baby.

Once more my Lady Dallia and I were together and now there were no more living enemies to trouble us ever again. A warrior of Rigel had brought his beloved lady home. The cities and people of our world were now free and safe.

As we neared the gleaming spires and towers of Asudra, my Lady Dallia and I rejoiced that we were finally free and would now be together forever. We had come through many dangers victoriously and now could live our lives in joy and happiness—and I knew I had become a true warrior of Rigel.

THE END

ABOUT OUR CREATORS

WRITER --

GARY LOVISI is the author of various stories that have appeared in Airship27 books over the years, including such quintessential pulp characters as The Moon Man, The Crimson Mask, The Purple Scar and The Phantom Detective. His latest books include *The Secret Adventures of Sherlock Holmes: Book Three* (Ramble House); and *Sherlock Holmes & Mr. Mac* (Stark House Press, Black Gat Book #11); as well as his popular 2012 Holmes novel for Airship27, *Sherlock Holmes: The Baron's Revenge*. He is a Mystery Writers of America Edgar Nominated author for his Sherlock Holmes story, "The Adventure of the Missing Detective." Lovisi has also written five books in his Jon Kirk of Ares series, a sword and fantasy series inspired by Edgar Rice Burroughs' John Carter of Mars books; with two new books in the series: #4 *The Mind Masters*, and #5 *The Time Masters*. His latest two books include *I, Barbarian* (Airship27, tpb), stories in the vein of Conan and Robert E. Howard; and *Weird Stories* (Ramble House, tpb) Horror/terror tales inspired by H.P. Lovecraft and Clark Ashton Smith." To find out more about Gary Lovisi and his books check out his website at www.gryphonbooks.com or visit him on Facebook and his video channel on YouTube.

COVER ARTIST--ILLUSTRATOR

RON HILL - has been an editorial cartoonist, humorous illustrator, graphic designer, educator, author, armchair theologian and video documentarian (not all at the same time, of course!) for over 40 years. Born in Cleveland, he graduated from the Art Institute of Pittsburgh and immediately returned to Northeast Ohio to begin working inadvertising.

In the 1980s–90s, as part of the illustration team of Lombardo & Hill, Ron drew countless interior illustrations for role-playing games published by TSR,

147

West End Games, Iron Crown Enterprises, and Chaosium, many involving licensed from The Lord of the Rings, Dungeons and Dragons, Indiana Jones and Star Wars. An accomplished quick-sketch caricature artist, he has drawn (to date) probably a quarter-million faces at thousands of private and public events from Chicago to New York. His editorial cartoons have appeared in the Chagrin Valley Times, Solon Times, Geauga Times Courier and West Life since 1999. In 2000 he started illustrating the popular "Armchair Theologian" book series for Westminster John-Knox; these 15 volumes have been translated into German, Japanese, Korean, Portuguese and Italian.

From 2002–2015, he taught an Interactive Media College Tech Prep program at Alliance High School, and has always conducted workshops at area art centers (including the Valley Art Center) since 1990. After co-founding Act 3, a media company and indie publisher in Cleveland in 2016, he has recently embarked (once again) on his solo career as a freelance artist, and is also currently working on a number of personal documentary projects, including"Go-Kart Therapy" and "We Are Doc Savage: A Documentary on Fandom." He has always lived in the Chagrin Valley of Northeast Ohio, and you can learn more at www.RonHillArtist.com.

He can be contacted and found here: ArtistRonHill@gmail.com • RonHillArtist.com

GLOSSARY

CRAGAS are foot long vicious fish with 3 rows of teeth, think barracudas.

HAAD is a unit of measurement, around 11-12' or close to one foot.

KULOTH a dangerous vicious small slithering reptile, lizard-like.

SQUAL a small rabbit-like plains animal, abundent and and a popular food.

SARCOTH appears at end of book, a man-eating, multi-fanged carnivore, lion or tiger-like. It has been made invisible when Tan fights it, but when he kills it, it becomes visible.

TAN OF ALVAKA – PRINCE OF ASUDRA

XO is a nasty insect about 6-8" in length but is a meat-eating giant ant-like creature.

ZIBAs are huge shaggy six-legged almost elephantine creatures with two rows of flat teeth, grass eaters, used for dray animals but a special breed of them are bred leaner for mounts for warriors. They are large and elephant like in size used as cavalry mounts.

AGE OF HEROES

"There once was an age of men before the dawn of pre-history, when magic ruled and heroic warriors fought with blood-drenched swords in vicious battles for treasure, power, and honor. It was a time undreamed of, far away in lost eons of time, where lived the most heroic men and women who had ever trod the earth under their momentous bold and brave hearts. In I, Barbarian, I try to recreate those adventures.

One such hero was Conan The Barbarian, created by Robert E. Howard. These incredible stories touched my heart and soul as a young man. They sang their songs boldly and honestly. Those stories, and others like them, by Howard, and other writers, made up my youth and are imbedded in my consciousness today — even so many decades later." From the Introduction by the author.

Gary Lovisi is one of New Pulp's most prolific and admired writers. Here, in this amazing collection, he offers eleven fast-paced, colorful pulp tales of mighty swordsmen, tempting witches, and dastardly wizards. Illustrated in inimitable style by Ron Hill! All of which are intended to make your blood race with the fever of High Adventure in the Age of Heroes.

Heroes of Legend

In this new collection, four classic heroes from mythology face new and dangerous challenges to prove once again their worthiness to claim the stature of legends. In the old world of the past, the Viking warrior Sigurd must battle overwhelming odds to attain Valhalla while Hercules travels to Hercules to seek the aid of the Red Sorceress.

Switching to the American frontier, the steel-driving man, John Henry encounters a blood-sucking monster ready to contaminate the West. Then Johnny Appleseed, walking the lad in his tin pot hat, comes to the aid of weary pioneers.

Here are four imaginative adventures from the pens of Teel James Glenn, Elizabeth Freeman, Eric Esquivel, Harding McFadden and Iris Hawkins. All beautifully illustrated by artist Ron Hill.

AN AIRSHIP 27 PRODUCTION

PULP FICTION FOR A NEW GENERATION!
Airship27Hangar.com

NEW PULP

VOLUME THREE

PULP MYTHOLOGY

FEATURING
John Henry Vs. the Vampires!

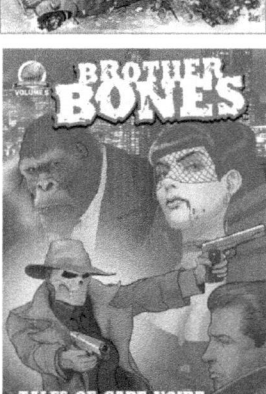